The Roar

BOOK ONE

A.M. WHITE

For my boys, I will love you long after this world is gone.

Chapter One

My eyes didn't want to open. If I opened them I would have to face my life all over again. Each day a reflection of the last, with the only differences being what was taken from us. Everyone knew that eventually we would be stripped of everything.

I sighed and sat up. I knew that if I didn't get up and head out to my assignment, I would lose even more the next time the Roar sounded. My feet tested the dirt floor. It was cold, but not wet today.

The cot creaked as I pulled on the dark jumpsuit and chunky boots that materialized after the sound took our own clothes. Our individual clothes were one of the last freedoms we allowed in this world.

As I tied my unruly hair on top of my head, I chanted my name five times, "Alex, Alex, Alex, Alex, Alex." It was part of my morning routine so that I wouldn't forget the way it sounded aloud. I hadn't heard my name spoken since the day the world ended.

No one cared about appearance anymore. We were all the same, slaves to the sound all around us. The Roar controlled everything.

I sighed and wondered if I would be given directions or have something taken next time. That was how it worked.

I grabbed my shovel and covered my eyes as the plywood door slammed shut behind me. My lunch pail sat on the ground exactly where it was every day.

The only people we ever saw were in our work crews. Sometimes that changed, but the job itself didn't. I figured that was the way it was; everyone worked within circles. It only made sense that there had to be people that prepared our food, replenished our cleaning stations, and of course, disposed of the unwanted people. There had to be an enormous invisible infrastructure to run a work camp this size.

We dug massive pits in the ground. Many left holes that waited for purpose. Some days, holes were filled with dirt. I tried to not think about the possibility that bodies might be hidden beneath the surface. The thought bothered me that I could have dug holes for people I knew, even my family.

I was assigned to dig on the south side of the plot. I was given the message yesterday, during the latest Roar. It was always the same in the beginning. Several repetitive booms spread and then a full-blown Roar wrapped around everything.

I didn't understand how the Roar found out when someone didn't follow instructions. No one ever told me what made the noise or where it came from.

A few other people dressed in jumpsuits emerged from their shacks lining the work zone. The land inside this area was cleared and barren. I kept my head down and listened to my boots as I crunched through the gravel and dirt. The morning was cool and nothing moved besides us. Birds and animals were never seen inside of the camp.

At the end of the plot, I looked down into a ditch. I was disheartened to know that my instructions were to dig until I hit bedrock. At least I knew that I wouldn't be taken anytime soon because this would be a long job. The people assigned the same job slowed as they came upon the hole. I am sure they felt the same weariness when they looked at the task ahead of us.

No one talked while we climbed and slid down the sides of the ditch to the bottom. I worked hard. Sweat ran down my back, even in the cool air. I heard the people around me as they worked.

It felt like someone watched me. Between strokes, I kept my head down, but darted my eyes around on alert. I wanted to do my job and go back to my little shack. My goal was to draw as little attention to myself as possible. If I could somehow get through this and die peacefully in my cot one night, I would be happy.

Some people lost it. They broke from everything taken. When they broke, it usually meant people died or disappeared. I had seen people lose their grip and become mad from the solitude and pressure.

The screams were terrible, like finger nails that tear at my skin. When that happened, there was nothing else in the world I wanted, but for it to stop.

I decided a long time ago that I'd rather die than disappear. Usually, if the person was able-bodied, they would be erased, never to be seen again. From time to time, an example was made of an attempted escapee or a person that refused to work. The mutilated body was displayed and tied to a spike in the work field for all to witness.

There was a man behind me. He watched my back as I worked. I felt it. I turned to the side and sized him up. I hadn't noticed him before.

His dark hair completely hid his eyes as he dug. His arms tensed each time he pulled the shovel from the ground. His jumpsuit matched mine, so nothing about him stood out as different. He seemed stable. There were no movements that flagged him as a threat.

I glanced over briefly and noticed his foot slide against the dirt to nudge a girl that worked at his side. That struck me as strange. It was one thing for a random person to lose their sanity, however, communication between workers was worse, especially if you cared about them. As a rule of thumb communication led to a disappearance not death.

I turned my back to them and continued to dig out the bottom of the pit. Not too fast, not too slow, just enough to not draw attention. Time always moved so slowly.

Digging was mundane business, but it made me stronger. My shoulders had broadened over the years and I found that I was able to put in a day's work without being too sore.

The silence gave me all the time I would ever need to sort my thoughts. I often drifted back through memories and recalled moments like pictures, so I wouldn't forget the way things once were. It was hard to believe that this world had been so different a few years ago.

The human-race went about our business. We tried to find happiness. We enjoyed choice with our families and friends. Humans had taken everything for granted. We polluted, pillaged, and blew each other up. It was our Earth and, for the most part, nations weren't held accountable for their own screw-ups. That was until the day the Earth woke up and we were all held accountable.

It began as a low rumble, only audible if you hushed the people in your vicinity. I remembered that I turned my head to the sound back then and hoped that someone else had heard it. If so, that meant I wasn't crazy. I wish I had been.

The Roar escalated until the thunder pulsed across the land and made people stop in their tracks. We all listened and waited with bated breath.

Once the people stopped to listen out of curiosity. Now, we all stopped, paralyzed by the sound, not in fear, but by the thunderous Roar emanated around us.

The sound demanded we stop. It wanted something from us.

I slowly climbed out of the hole. I dug my boots into the grit and used my shovel to pull myself up. The pit was over my head in depth. We made a dent in the Earth.

I noticed the man scrambled clumsily from the side before the girl popped out. He walked quickly, but not too far ahead of her. They seemed to know each other, not just from the nudge I had witnessed, but as though they were something to each other. That was dangerous business.

I felt it then, the first rumble in a series. Someone near me gasped. Was it the girl from the hole? I dropped my shovel. I learned to drop it away before the last Roar to avoid injury.

Another louder boom rang out and several other shovels hit the ground around me. I guess they had all gone through the same lesson at some point. My eyes scanned the ground to make sure I would not end up bruised on anything.

Then the final Roar came. I felt it in my legs, it held me still. A fire began inside of me. It ran from the ground up my spine and into my head. Screams swirled around me. I wasn't sure if they came from my mouth or others around me.

The pain blinded me and seared through my brain. Just when I thought it would kill me, it stopped, and left me in silent darkness. Words came through the darkness and red flashes spelled out instructions. My mind caught each word and ran them together. The last word flashed in my mind and I felt my eyes slowly creep open.

"Stay in the south plot tomorrow night." The words placed themselves in order as I rolled into a seated position. I breathed out heavily. "More work!" I thought. That meant no sleep tomorrow night.

Everyone stood and continued to their shacks. I scanned the area quickly to see if anyone was taken.

The young man and the girl were gone. I stood and took longer than I should have to search the plot for their dark hair. There was no sign of them.

Chapter Two

I opened the cabinet; the only cabinet in the shack and found my dinner wrapped in a cloth napkin. It was there every night, just as my lunch in the mornings. My mind flitted for a second and I wondered how it got there.

My eyes squeezed shut. I shook the question out of my head.

I didn't care how it appeared. I only cared that it was there. I plopped on the edge of the cot and greedily opened the satchel. I stared at the standard biscuits and dried meat.

The tough meat and stale bread hardly got chewed as I choked it down. I tore the last biscuit and noticed something fall to the ground. I bent close to the floor, while I tried to swallow the hard bread in my mouth. I retrieved the object. I did not look closely at it. It was slippery between my fingers and moist from humidity in the satchel. I held a thin piece of paper.

I remembered paper. We had it before the Roars began. It was among the first things taken away. I could only guess it was because we communicated with it. Then all technology went, so there was no way for anyone to communicate across any distance. Humanity became isolated.

Next, all modes of transportation ceased to function. Cars littered every road and highway. They were frozen in time and abandoned by survivors.

Luckily, planes were grounded when the technology went away, so they didn't fall from the sky. The fear of that terrified me.

After that, the land was broken into sectors and we were quarantined with instructions during Roars. In the beginning, a lot of people tried to not listen. They tried to run and were either found dead or just disappeared altogether. That worked as a very persuasive way to get the rest of us to comply.

The paper felt so thin in my fingers. I could barely remember the feel of it. There were markings on it, I felt the indentations. The edges were torn roughly. It was a small bit torn from a larger piece. I pulled it close to my eyes and stopped to listen for any reason to not unfold it. Silence was my only company.

I flattened it in my hand. I noticed the calluses from the shovel on my fingers and palms. For a second, a picture of my thin and soft hands flashed in my mind. I guessed the old me remained buried somewhere inside and I couldn't forget.

Sometimes I wanted to forget it all, my family, the way they looked the last time I saw them, the way I looked in a mirror, and our home; its warm embrace around me. I needed to forget, to survive times when it was too hard to bear. I shook off the thoughts that distracted me.

I read the paper. "I will be there tomorrow night."

I tossed it in my mouth, quickly, in case I was watched. I hoped that if anyone watched it looked like a bit of the biscuit fell from my meal.

I took a deep breath and went about business as usual.

Questions ran through my head. "What was this? Why was someone going to be there? Did this have anything to do with the man and the girl?"

I shook the jumpsuit off. I recalled the footprints in the dirt that headed toward the woods on the outskirts of the camp. I splashed water on my face from the basin in the corner of the room. The basin water was refreshed daily, but there was no inclination of how it came to be there. I didn't want to know. I told myself again. It was part of my routine. The routine was safe. The message was not part of the routine, which made it inherently dangerous.

I pushed the note from my thoughts. I had to stay alive. I could not do something dangerous. Someone, somewhere would make it end. I was only a small pawn in a much larger game.

I stared at the wall, a term I used loosely, as I had for years and waited for sleep to come. I crawled onto the cot and pulled the burlap sheet over my shoulder. It scratched my neck as I turned on my side. Thank goodness, the tight shirt and leggings protected the rest of me from the burlap. I recalled the first nights I had to use it. Something as little as the loss of my own blankets had kept me awake several nights until I succumbed to exhaustion.

Chapter Three

I shivered beneath my scratchy cover. I couldn't force sleep back anymore. Dreams came; they barged in as I knew they would. At first, they were memories, just moments caught in time, a birthday party with friends, a hug from my mother, sitting in class taking notes.

Then my mother was on the phone to me. She told me to run and go to our house. Home wasn't far away from my apartment. Then she screamed. The memory of her scream, it was almost more painful than the screams that surrounded me during the Roar.

It was night. I was on the road. I drove as fast as I could. I scanned every radio station in the area. I heard nothing but static. The moon looked like it dripped blood. Scripture of the apocalypse nagged at me, this would be the end of us all.

I swerved to miss holes that were opened in the pavement. The Earth moved beneath me.

The neighborhood was in chaos. Many of the homes were on fire. People dragged each other from them. Screams echoed in the air.

My home was no longer there. All that remained were ashes. I saw charred bodies from my car among the ruins, and smoke still rose from what used to be our home. I fumbled to open the door and fell onto the asphalt. The stench of burned bodies filled my nose.

I couldn't handle it. I had to wake up.

Someone ran to the car.

"Please help me!"

A person tried to shove me out of the way. I kicked them as hard as possible and climbed back inside. A boy's hand grabbed the door to keep it open. I struggled against him. Somehow, I managed to get back into the seat. Then I remembered the multi tool my dad gave me in the console.

He screamed at me. "Get out of the car! I swear to God, I will kill you!"

I looked at his face for the first time and it was my neighbor's son. He yanked on the door. I strained against his strength. I gripped the pliers in my hand and shoved them into the boy's arm. Blood spurt everywhere and he let go of the door.

The dream moved to another place and time. I was in my house again. I sat in a corner and rubbed an old scar on my shin. It itched like crazy and distracted me from an unknown urgency inside. I looked at the old scar. I couldn't remember how I got it, but it looked more irritated than usual. It was a red streak along the bone of my shin.

There were no phones, no radio, no car, no running water, no electricity, no television, no computers, or any other technology. I ran from one luxury to the next, tried it and found it was no longer there.

How am I here? I saw the house burned to the ground. Then the sound and the Roar followed to explain the illusion of the house and that things had been taken. I cried heavily, which is how I submitted, every time. The nightmares never relented.

Everything after that was a chain of repetition. I lived through the pain of the Roar. Memories of my past and the freedoms taken until we had no more plagued me.

Among the redundant days that followed people cracked and lost their minds, which resulted in either a disappearance or a Roar. Often a body left as proof of the power held over us. The shock and panic was left behind on cold faces.

I don't even wake from the nightmares anymore. Of course, I am always scared. The pain is enough to remind me why I stay in line.

It seemed that not many people made it through the beginning, at least, not from what I could tell in my sector. I hoped there were other sectors with people. There was still a small glimmer of hope that somewhere out there, someone I knew might be alive. I pushed that hope down deep. I didn't want to care, because that causes more pain.

I woke in the morning at the same time I did every day with beads of sweat on my brow. Every morning I wake to find I am still in a part of that nightmare.

Tiny rows of sunlight squeezed through the slats of my shack. The light was pretty. It cascaded down the back of my hand and gave it a golden glow. I felt a smile start to swell and shoved it back down inside me.

I turned my hand over and the beams highlighted the dirt permanently ground into the lines of my palm. It reminded me of why I shouldn't allow myself to feel happiness. I peeled the burlap from my skin to start my day again.

Chapter Four

The air became cooler. When I stepped out of the shack, it almost took my breath away. I picked up my lunch pail from the stoop and started to head to the ditch. Once I began to work I would feel warmer. I tugged on the ends of my sleeves and tried to pull my hands inside a bit. My fingers seemed to stay cold.

Other footsteps joined mine as the workers moved to their stations. Some dragged their shovels that made a scraping sound on the ground. I wondered if that made them look weak to whoever watched us.

I didn't want to look weak. The sick and weak didn't last long before they were replaced with a newer, younger, healthier person.

Suddenly, my attention snapped to the sound of footsteps that approached from behind. Before long, the steps were in sync with mine and closer than I found comfortable. No one had been this close to me in years and I couldn't see the person that would dare. I turned my head to seem like I looked at the sun's position. That was safe.

It was him, the man from the day before, only a full pace behind me. His head was turned down, so I couldn't make out his face, but the figure belonged to him. The girl that accompanied him yesterday didn't seem to be with him.

I picked up speed, ready to get to the ditch where this man would have to stay busy, and I could find places away from him to dig. I already knew I wanted to be on the end. I could stay out of the way and hopefully that man, whoever he was, would get the hint and back off. I could put my back to the other diggers. That way, I would be aware of my surroundings.

The alcove blocked the wind, but it was considerably more damp and cool. I remembered my mom telling me to not go out in the rain when I was little because I would get sick. Being damp and cold all winter was not good for our health.

"I won't get sick." I told myself. "I can't."

I had been sick before out there. I had worked, sweating from fever, weak, or even as I coughed into my arm to silence the hacking from others. Thank God, that hadn't happened too often, because it tested me. There had been times I almost gave up and didn't get out of bed in the morning even though I knew it meant I would be gone very soon.

With each ram of the shovel, puffs of my breath escaped and floated away. My eyes watched my breath drift from the ditch and get lost in the sky above. I wondered if that is how our soul leaves the body.

Digging had become such a second nature to me, I became a machine. I could dig all day and not really think about digging.

Someone behind me coughed. It was a wet noise that gurgled and made me cringe. A rattling cough wasn't a good sign. I didn't turn to see where it came from. I didn't care.

The hours passed and my stomach began to grip at my thoughts. Food was only one of the few necessities we kept. Generally, the food was bland, dried, and small portioned. All the workers grew lean from the diet and labor, but the food was enough to survive. Not much work could be done without calorie intake.

As if on cue, we all stopped and climbed the edges of the hole for lunch. It was more difficult to get to the top the further we dug. I grabbed my metal pail and found a spot away from the others to settle myself. I never understood why some of the people sat closely during our ten-minute lunch allowance. People weren't allowed to talk and even if they tried, out here in the open, that would be stupid.

I pulled the cloth that wrapped my dried fruit and crackers out and placed it between my legs.

The canteen, tucked in to the bottom, was what I wanted. My hands were shaking from the work and my mouth was parched. I dropped the cap beside me and guzzled the water as fast as I could.

That was when he came and sat next to me. I could truly see that he was alone today.

He took out his wrapped lunch and canteen. He gulped down the water the same as me. I closed my eyes and permitted myself to enjoy the feel of it briefly, before I decided what to do about this guy. He had begun to make himself a little too comfortable in my presence.

I put the lid on my canteen and slammed it on the ground between us. His eyes found mine instantly. They were different than I had ever seen before. The look on my face had been meant to be a warning, to back off, but those eyes caught me off guard. I forced myself to look down at my lap and not stare. My breath picked up speed as I tried to process what I had seen. His eyes were black, the whole thing. There was no white, no color, only black. I wondered if I had finally lost my mind.

The man turned to his meal. I heard him chew and swallow the tough food. My hand instinctively brought some of my food to my mouth. I realized that I had only paid attention to his eyes. I had not made a point to look at his face. I tried to shift my eyes so that I could get a good look without turning my whole head. His hair fell in his face as he ate. If I waited till he lifted his head. I could pretend to drop a crumb of food and catch a glimpse while I retrieved it.

Before I knew it, I had nervously ingested most of the lunch. I kept one eye on him and tried to act normal. The meal seemed even shorter than usual. I saved a small morsel for the right moment. He hadn't lifted his head at all. He stared into his lap while he ate. He rolled the empty cloth and placed it in his pail.

A hand lifted to his eyes, head still low, but I could tell he was going to run his fingers through his pitch-black hair. His hair matched his eyes.

I dropped the crumb and quickly moved to retrieve it just at the second his hand pulled the drape of hair back from his face, on my side. His profile was distinct, with a sharp nose and squared jawline. The muscles under his skin clenched as I quickly analyzed him. I plucked the food from the ground and quickly tossed it in the bucket.

He was younger than I had thought. He was only a few years older than myself. I assumed he was older because there was something about the way he moved made him seem more confident than most people my age.

In unison, our group finished lunch and found our way back down to our work areas. I couldn't keep my mind here and now.

Was it possible he had pulled back his hair on purpose so that I could get a better look at him? If

I could hear him chew and swallow during lunch, he could probably hear my breath became more rapid after I saw his eyes. Why had he shown me? What was he?

I looked at my white knuckles on the end of the shovel and forced my grip to relax. As weird as this was it wasn't worth the blisters later.

The mud behind me sloshed as he trudged up close from the other side of several workers. He dropped his shovel and it clattered to the ground.

He bent down and upon retrieval quickly slid something into the pocket of my jumpsuit.

He paused for a moment to lock eyes with me once more. The eyes of obsidian weren't figments of my imagination. There they were, right in front of me, plain as day. A puff of breath escaped me only to be quickly sucked back in with a muffled gasp.

I listened and waited for someone to notice the exchange. I half expected to feel the Earth move under me and to meet my end. No one would ever get away with trying to communicate. I had seen people try to speak in hushed whispers as they walked to their work positions. One minute they were there, and after a roar, they were gone as if they never existed. No one left to think about them much less talk about them.

I leaned against the side of one wall and used one hand to dig while I felt around in my pocket with the free hand. The paper was smooth between my fingers and already flattened. He must have known I wouldn't have two hands to unravel the note down here.

In one swift movement, I read the short message. "We will talk tonight".

I popped it into my mouth. There would be no evidence that I had anything to do with the freak beside me. He saw me read and then dispose of the note. A small grin was on his lips; just visible in my periphery.

Anxiety took hold of me and time passed even slower than normal in this hell. The dark-eyed man worked next to me the whole day. He never tried to communicate or get my attention again. I noticed the veins on the back of his hands and that they were considerably larger than my own, wrapped around the handle of his shovel. His breath seemed calmer and slower than my own, even as the day passed. I wondered what kind of work he normally did, if this came so easy to him.

The sun finally drifted out of view. Our team had made a large dent in the Earth. The time came when everyone else stopped working and used the shovels to knock out pieces of dirt along the wall to make stairs so they could climb out of the depths.

Last night's message was clear, I was meant to stay and work throughout the night. Now that this thing was the only one left with me, I had to consider other options.

If I stayed, he might kill me, or worse. I might have dug my own grave the last couple of days. If I decided to climb out of the ditch and disobey orders, I would die or disappear.

We worked in silence for quite a while. The sun sank lower into the sky and the shadows grew longer. I imagined them swallowing me like a monster that had been waiting for a sacrifice. People shuffled by above, some grunted, a few raggedly coughed, many pulled their shovels along the ground behind them which scratched against the gravel and gritty soil.

Finally, there was no more noise from above me. Only the sounds of the two of us alive and working echoed in the cavity. My stomach felt sick and my hands were slippery with sweat. If he was going to kill me I just wanted it over with quickly.

He paused and turned his head to make sure there was no one above us. I slowed my pace and turned to try and make out the details of him in the darkness. Only a sliver of moon provided any light. Before I could adjust my eyes, he had me pinned on the ground. His elbows ground my arms into the mud, knees pressed against my thighs, and hands covered my mouth.

I tried to scream but the air surged from my chest only to be blocked and muffled. He had complete control over me.

“Sshhhh, sshhhh, I’m not going to hurt you.” He repeated in a soft whisper that grazed my cheek.

I squirmed beneath his weight. His face was so close to mine, his breath smelled like the earth. I could finally see his face in entirety. Nothing about it was scary, except the eyes. They were inches from mine and looked like pools of ink staring through me.

I felt my death was certain now. I had seen television shows before the world ended; murders and what men do to women when they have them pinned to the ground. The ground crumbled under my fingers and the dampness of it soaked my back. Adrenaline poured through my body with nowhere to go.

"I promise. I swear to you that I will not do any harm to you." His hands did not loosen. "Do you hear me?" He looked in my eyes for some acknowledgement.

I nodded the best I could. My teeth pierced my lips. I tasted blood.

"Good girl. I hate this part. You people always look at me that way when I'm trying to save you. I need a moment to explain and then I will let go. If you scream, I will be gone before they Roar. They will not take me. Do you understand?" His eyes searched mine again.

I struggled against him once more. Irritating pain and a numbing sensation crawled through my lower leg. The pressure of him hurt. He must've seen it in my eyes, because he eased up a bit.

"I am here to save you." He stopped for a second when he saw my eyes darting around, waiting for something to come from above.

He grinned. "They can't hear us whisper or see us this far down. They only put the trusted ones down this deep, because they know you obey." He let this settle into my thoughts.

"Tell them you were knocked unconscious. Someone kicked you." He instructed.

My brain tried to register everything, to make connections of whether he told the truth. I tried to think over the sound as I heaved for air.

Every time the Roar happened I was above standing on the ground in the open or in my shack. Maybe this was a truth.

He released me and was gone before I could speak.

Chapter Five

I had never seen a person move the way he did. He scaled the wall like an animal. Fear ran through my body and I dragged myself to sit with my back pressed to the wall.

Footsteps came and a girl peered over the ledge. Her eyes widened when she saw me with my hair and eyes wild.

"What are you doing?" Her voice was sharp. I was sure she had experienced a Roar for the instructions to come and find me. Her being mean was excused due to the pain she endured.

I gave her the excuse that my attacker had given me. I was fine now and the kick had just taken a few minutes for me to get over.

She huffed, but gave me the end of a shovel and pulled me out. I sprawled on the ground, my own shovel beside me.

"Get up. I am supposed to walk you to your shack." She turned on her heels and marched away.

I scrambled to keep up and touched my forehead a few times to make my story more believable. My shin throbbed, so I limped as I walked.

I recognized her as a girl that worked the most northern rim of the field. She must be a trusted one, because she was made to dig deep trenches like the one I worked.

Questions and thoughts rattled inside of me, but I knew not to talk, kept my head down, and focused on breathing normally. This girl was like me, a rule follower. When she was asked about how she found me, she would tell them exactly what she saw.

We reached the shed. She asked, "Will you be okay to work tomorrow?"

I gave her the most confident, "Yes," I could and walked inside. I was glad for my long jumpsuit, there had to be marks from my attacker holding me down. They would have been obvious signs that my alibi was a lie.

Inside, the shack seemed lonelier than ever. It would take time to process everything that happened. I was relieved that he hadn't asked me to make a choice immediately.

The world spun uncontrollably at the violence to my body. I hadn't been touched in years. Not to mention I heard another person talk. On this night I heard two voices and that was overwhelming.

I went about my normal routine. I ate in my jumpsuit, stripped my outer layer, and readied for bed.

I looked under my shirt to see the dark bruises of the assault already formed while I analyzed what the man had said.

He said so much in such a short amount of time. Someone out there wanted me. To take such a chance, they must have believed I would decide to leave. Memories of my family tugged at this thought, but I had seen them all dead, what was left of them anyway.

If the man had wanted to kill me, or worse, he could have in the hole. I had seen how quickly he could move, and I had reminders of his strength on my skin. His prowess and capability scared me.

I weighed the fear of staying in this place over leaving. I could be taken tomorrow at the whim of whoever controlled the Roar. I was theirs if I stayed. There was no escaping an end, but I could decide how my end would come. With that thought sleep came.

The next morning came in the blink of an eye. My eyes felt swollen and my bruises ached. A funny thought came to me, that if I ever saw that man again I wanted punch him square in his face, because he made me feel like this. I smirked at the thought; he was my secret. This was a pain that didn't leave like the one that came with the Roar and I held him accountable.

"When would he come again?" I asked myself.

He had said, "Tomorrow," with no details as to what hour. My mind had better be made up in case it was sooner than later. I believed I already had my mind made up. He was a chance to not disappear, either by death or from being used more than I was already.

What bothered me was his aggression. It made me question his intentions. In addition, I would lose what I knew to go to something unknown. There were certain things I could control here; I knew I would be fed, have shelter, and have a job. Beyond our sector, if there was even a beyond, I had no idea what I would find.

All these thoughts irked me until I ended up at the ledge of the trench. I looked down into the darkness and I resolved to leave this place. There could be nothing as despairing and ominous as the pit that lay in front of me. I was ordered every day to dig for our masters. It would never end. There was no explanation or rationale to this. I dug whatever and whenever they wanted.

It was then, right before any of us began our decent to the bottom that the ground shook. I dropped my shovel away from my body. I leaned backwards and hoped I would fall away from the edge.

The pain I knew so well took a hold of me. "All will work till sun down from now on. Make sure to leave no one behind."

As I stirred, face down, I knew the instructions had been made because of me. The excuse I had made for my accident had been relayed. The masters had decided to not let that happen again and by some grace, I was still here.

They must have believed me. There was no reason not to. I had always done what was asked of me and never strayed from normality. I thanked the dark-eyed man silently.

My hand went to my head, to keep up the story about getting kicked. Someone had placed a ladder down in the ditch. It would be easier to get down and back up at the end of the day. My injury had been answered with a ladder. Down we went, one by one, to our daytime sentence.

The day dragged on just like any other. Every so often, I stopped and looked around for the man. He said he would come today for my answer, but with no inclination as to what time, put me on edge. Lunch came and went, it was useless to try and eat.

Finally, the time came for all of us to head back to our shacks. The shovel felt heavier than usual. Being out in the open, I could feel my body become tense. I hoped he would be inconspicuous upon his arrival. I wanted to get into the safety of my own space.

My routine continued until I was in my bed. Every noise sent an alert signal to my brain. Still the was no sign of him. I began to wonder if he would come back.

"Had he been caught? Was this some kind of test?" I cursed myself for the hope that I allowed into my life, even if it was short lived.

I lay on the scratchy cot and stared at the boards. Sleep escaped me, because I couldn't shut off my self-loathing. I imagined running through the woods alongside the man. Each person that could be on the other side flashed through my head.

I saw family members that could have escaped. I come from strong stock, people that know how to survive. That was what crushed me the most about seeing the burned bodies in my home. They should've known better than to cling to each other in an emergency like that.

I saw movement between the slats in the boards. It halted my day dream and I got goosebumps, was it him? The shadows moved low trying to situate between boards.

"Alex?" A ragged whisper broke through the darkness. "Alex?"

I sat up and put my hand against a crack close the shadow.

"Until your feet touch the ground, they can't hear you, just whisper. Have you made up your mind?" The voice asked.

I nodded. "Who wants me to come with you?"

"I can't tell you, you just have to decide." His shadow on the other side crouched even further. "I need an answer, now."

"Yes." I croaked.

"Then run. Run to me, I will carry you from here." His urgency told me I had to hurry.

My feet hit the floor, I sprinted to the door; he stood there waiting for me. He swung me onto his back.

We moved at a speed that I could not comprehend. He moved in such and animalistic way.

We passed the back of the shack, over the barbed wire fence, and then into the trees that lined our sector. I was wrapped around him and held on for dear life.

No one had ever made it past the fence. I heard people try to climb it. The clinking sound was unmistakable, but was always followed with a Roar. Then the mutilated bodies of the attempted escapees were dragged into the field and displayed to deter the rest of us from trying to escape.

I clung to him. He had complete control and I had to trust him with my life. I decided that when I agreed to leave. Either I would die or live; it was a fifty/ fifty chance with him. By leaving, that choice was better than the hundred percent that I would die if I stayed.

At times, he leaned forward and moved on all fours. We reached a fallen tree where he grabbed my legs around his middle to make sure I was secure before he effortlessly bounded over it. Everything was silent, except the rhythm of his feet. It was apparent that he had transported people like this before.

The trees whizzed by. Every now and again, a branch would clip my arms. Each hit was a surprise, because of the darkness. It hurt terribly; I bit down on my lip to keep from making noise due to the pain.

The Roar did come, but too late. I could hear it but I no longer felt it. We were beyond its reach. I looked over my shoulder and no longer saw any sign of the compound.

"It won't be much longer till we can take a break. We aren't totally in the clear just yet." He paused to shift my weight.

His muscles contracted with each movement and I realized how strong he was. I wondered if his abnormal strength and the color of his eyes had something to do with each other.

There was the sound of water ahead. When we met the source, my stomach dropped. The river in front of us swirled around jagged rocks and dared anything to test its force. The water looked alive in the silver moonlight.

We stopped and he readjusted me. "On the other side we will be able to rest a minute. I need you to stay quiet and hold on till we get over there, ok?" He urged.

I nodded and sank into his back.

"I can make it on the rocks." He panted.

He took a few steps back to get a running start. My breath lodged in my throat. He shot off toward the bank. The moment his feet left the ground my eyes locked shut. Each rock landing jarred my bones and shoved the air out of me a little more. I squeezed him hard enough that it hurt. The final landing was slightly more graceful and he lifted me from his back to set me on the ground. My knees wobbled, my body threatened to crumple.

"You ok?" He steadied me.

I stumbled to the nearest bush and dry heaved. My body convulsed and I sank to the ground.

"Good Lord, Alex, I thought I was better at this stuff than that." He stood over me, his black eyes ominous.

"I'm sorry. I-I thought I was tougher than that," I looked up at him.

He laughed and produced a water bladder from beneath his shirt. "Here, you need to drink some and I need to refill this while we are here."

I crawled to a tree and leaned against it. The water was cool and felt amazing in my throat. I watched him crouch by the water and fill a spare bladder.

"What's your name?" I asked.

"Timothy." He took the bag from me and returned to the river. "Don't ask about my eyes or how I move the way I do. I won't answer you, at least not yet. We have a few days trek ahead of us and that discussion won't help either of us right now."

He helped me to my feet.

"Where are we going?" I asked.

"Home, someone there contracted me to find you," he answered.

Timothy paced the edges of the path.

"Someone paid you to find me?" My heart skipped a beat.

"Someone paid me very well to find you."

"Who did?" I breathed.

"I don't know. I never do business directly with the hire. It's better for everyone that way." He pointed to his eyes as if that explained why.

Timothy rummaged in a bush nearby and produced a pair of boots and a jacket for each of us. He dropped the boots and black leather jacket in front of me.

"These should fit. I'm glad you forgot your own; it would have meant lost time for us. You have to wear these boots any time your feet are on the ground."

"Why?" I asked, pulling the boots on quickly. I noticed they were heavier than the ones from camp.

"Let's just say they can't see you through the ground with them on; luckily they can't reach you with their messages either. See, I have a pair too."

He looked down. "I don't really need them like you do, but better safe than sorry. Once we get home it won't really matter because their machines don't reach that far."

He pulled on his jacket. It was red, but faded from wear. Our eyes met and he explained the red. "Our enemies can't see red but our friends can. The color will signal that we are friendly so they won't kill us." I pursed my lips.

"You people never talk much at first. I hope you become a better travel partner than this." A smirk crossed his face.

Timothy walked to the other side of the path and lifted a rock. In one fluid motion, he tucked a gun down the back of his pants.

"There isn't one for you. I don't want you to decide I'm not a good travel partner and off me. We have to move; it's not good to stay anywhere too long this close to the compound."

Timothy turned and walked through the trees. I was glad he didn't expect me to keep up with his prior pace. That would be impossible.

Chapter Six

I realized quickly that I sounded like a bull in a China shop in the woods. I smiled, that was something my mom would say about me. "Miss Grace," she called me, because of my clumsiness.

I learned to follow his steps. Timothy made absolutely no noise and moved with ease.

Eventually, we came to an area where the pines turned into more leafy trees. He lifted a hand for me to stop. His head turned and he listened in every direction.

A shadowy figure dropped to the ground in front of us. Timothy's hand went to the gun at his back.

"Hey." A small voice announced. I hid behind Timothy.

"Seriously, Cara, I told you not to freaking do that!" Timothy scolded.

She shoved past him. "So, this is her?" She looked me up and down. "She better be worth the trouble."

The frail girl eyed me; her stark, midnight eyes lifted to mine when she stood on tippy toes. I took a step back. She was the girl that had accompanied him the first time in the trench.

"I'm glad to see you didn't tell her, this time. Last time it was such a mess." She poked at him. I noticed the knife at her side. She also wore a red hoodie.

He grumbled. "Nice to see you, too." He turned to me. "Don't worry about Cara, she lacks social skills."

Cara was small in frame but she made up for it in gumption. She turned and punched Timothy in the arm.

"No, I just don't care for this business like you." Cara sneered. She walked ahead.

"She is my partner," he explained. "She's a pain in the neck, but a good person to have on your side."

Timothy followed in the direction Cara had gone. I sighed and went along.

I knew my place; I am at the mercy of these people. Both of my chaperones were armed and I had nothing. Both had on red, which apparently flagged them as safe to others. My black jacket made me question how people would perceive me.

I wasn't too thrilled that it seemed Cara wasn't fully on board with the deal that was struck. I hoped that whoever was paying them paid enough for her to not hand me over, if it came to that. The epiphany of the situation hadn't exactly calmed me.

The forest made noises around us. It wasn't like at the sector where I never saw a bird or heard anything but the sounds of other people and the Roar.

A crack of wood in the distance made us all stop and bend low. We waited to see if it was a natural noise.

We walked for what seemed an hour. Finally, we came to a huge tree with low branches. Cara climbed it right away.

Timothy grabbed my arm. "We are sleeping here tonight. There is a platform up there."

"Ok." I squeaked. I remembered his comment about people like me not talking much.

"You first." He whispered.

I clung to the nearest branch and pulled myself up. The limbs were like a ladder. I was thankful for the upper body strength I had acquired from digging. I thought it was funny how you can be thankful for things like that. I was glad it was still dark, so I couldn't see how far up the tree I had climbed. I was not particularly fond of heights.

When I reached the platform, Cara lounged against the trunk and drank from a bladder of her own. I crawled forward and leaned against the trunk also. Timothy leapt to us from a few branches below. He landed gracefully on his feet.

Cara gave him a nasty look. “Show off.”

Timothy looked unfazed.

“You will probably want to sleep right where you are. We can’t afford you falling during the night.” Cara pointed at me. She curled up on the boards.

“Here.” Timothy handed me a water bladder. “Hold on to this from now on.”

He sat between Cara and me. He looked me over. I am sure he saw fear in my eyes.

“I always mean what I say; I am sure this is overwhelming to you but I promise to deliver you. I have lost people before that couldn’t handle life out here. You are going to be stronger than that, right?” He raised an eyebrow at me.

Cara piped up. “You better not lose her, and she is worth a good bit, Timothy.”

He sighed, “You better try and get some rest. We have a long day ahead of us.” He settled on his back.

I looked up at the sky and tried to get comfortable.

Chapter Seven

It seemed that I had just fallen asleep when a hand clamped over my mouth. My eyes shot open; my breath ragged from alarm. It was still night and hard to make out shapes. Timothy was on me. His finger signaled me to be quiet. He pointed below where footsteps crackled on dried leaves. Flashlight's danced around the canopy above.

He kept his hand pressed to my lips while he shifted over me to lay face down on the boards. He peered between the slats to get a better look at our unwelcome visitors. My eyes caught Cara in the same position and made fast hand signals to Timothy.

He leaned in to my ear and whispered no louder than a breath. "They don't see us."

I nodded even though it didn't make sense. How did they not see the platform this close?

The crunch of leaves and sticks continued to move away from us. I relaxed a little and strained to listen to the sounds below. There were probably four people that moved slowly in a grid like pattern through the forest. I could only guess they were a search committee sent to find me. Eventually, their sounds faded in the distance.

Cara groaned and curled back into sleep. Timothy scooted away from me and released his hand from my mouth.

"They were looking for me, weren't they?" I shook with fear.

"No, they were looking for us." He turned his back to me.

The reality and fear I felt gripped me. A single tear rolled down my cheek and ran into my hair. Fear began to channel into anger. I was so angry at myself that I wanted to cry. I was angry that I was hiding in a tree from something I had never seen. Heat flushed my skin. I made the decision then for no more tears, one was too many.

Morning came and left us all stiff and still exhausted. I think we all slept with one eye open after the search party came through.

"How did they not see us?" I asked.

They both looked at me because my voice sounded strange even to me.

"There were people sent out here to find you. People usually don't try too hard to find their own kind. There is a part of them that is glad you got out. They will probably have a meal withheld since they didn't recover you, not a big deal." Cara handed out dry biscuits for breakfast. We all sat in silence and inhaled the food. When we finished, we descended from the tree.

"If we move at a decent pace, we might just make it to a nicer spot to sleep tonight." Timothy tried to sound hopeful.

Cara moaned. "A place we can bathe." She pointed at me. "Alex, you are going to keep up with us today because I am going to take a bath tonight."

I eagerly nodded. Wash myself? That sounded heavenly. I could keep up with them for that.

The walk was pleasant. The morning light seemed to make everything glow. Winter had set in and it grew cooler as the days passed. Light frost was sprinkled around the forest floor. After a while animals began to wake and join in the chorus of life.

The sun gave me a chance to finally get my bearings. We moved south. I had no idea where we were or where we came from, this knowledge gave me back my sense of direction.

When the world had ended, I had been relocated to my sector. There had been no explanation as to my new whereabouts.

I reached forward and tugged on Timothy. "Where are we?" I asked.

He paused. "Well, this was near the Georgia-Carolina border." He stuffed his hands in his pockets and waited to see my reaction.

"Wow." I had been transported a few hundred miles to dig trenches.

Timothy pulled my arm so that I moved in sync with him. "They always move people. That way nothing seems familiar and it makes people more afraid to escape."

I replied. "That makes sense."

"Most of what they do makes sense. I mean, if you are trying to enslave a species and suck their world dry and all." He looked at my face.

"Do you mean they aren't human?" I already had my suspicions.

"I think you are a smart girl and have already figured that one out." The edge of his mouth twitched.

"I think you are right, but I'm not sure I'm ready to face that." I regarded him.

Some questions were being answered, but each answer seemed to create more questions.

Cara walked in front, as usual. She seemed completely uninterested in our conversation. I couldn't blame her for being rude. Here she was risking her life to free a stranger, even if she was getting paid. I was still a stranger that knew nothing about how the world had changed.

"Until I can get a grip on everything, I am only going to ask questions that I can deal with knowing the answer to, okay?" I added.

I raised an eyebrow. There was too much to comprehend and I knew I was fragile.

"That makes perfect sense. From my side, I will only answer questions I think you can handle for now." He held his hand out to me.

I shook his hand. "That's a deal."

Cara screamed and disappeared suddenly in front of us. We stopped dead in our tracks. I looked to Timothy for how to react. He sprang forward, pulled the gun from his pants and held it at his side. At the place she disappeared there was a narrow slice in the ground.

"Cara? Cara!" He yelled.

Timothy panicked and bent at the crevice to try to see her. There was no answer. He yanked off his jacket and belt.

"I've got to get down there, quickly. This is a trap, see the branches and leaves?" He nodded at the brush used to camouflage the hole.

I grabbed his shoulder and said, "The opening is too narrow for you. I have to go down."

He looked at me and at the mouth of the hole. I could see the struggle in his mind.

"It won't do anyone any good if you get stuck in there," I reasoned.

Timothy sighed, "Okay, I am going to strap my belt and jacket around you so that I can lower you down." He worked to rig a contraption that would hold me.

My legs dangled into the crevice. I slid into the crack, my feet reached for the bottom. The belt gave me a tug when Timothy caught my weight. The crack opened to a larger cavern.

"I think it's just a little lower, I'm going to release myself." I called up to him.

With a thud, I hit the bottom.

A dark shadow huddled against the wall. I felt my way to her.

"Cara, come on Cara." I shook her and she answered with a grunt.

"Alex, is she alright?" Timothy yelled down to me.

I quickly checked her over. She was a little scratched up and had been knocked out, but was alive.

"I think so!" I replied.

I took out the water bladder and poured it onto Cara's face. She stirred.

Disoriented, she mumbled. "Ugh, what the heck?" I helped her sit up.

"Are you okay?" I grabbed at her arms and legs checking to make sure there were no broken bones.

"What an idiot! I can't believe I fell for that!" She exclaimed and leaned onto me to stand straight.

"I hate to interrupt you ladies but the trappers could come back any moment. We yelled enough for anyone within a mile to hear us. We have to get somewhere discreet, fast!" Timothy urged.

I grabbed the end of the belt and wrapped it around both of her wrists. I buckled it for good measure.

"Hang on, tight." I patted her back. "She's ready!"

Cara inched toward the opening. Dirt fell into my face as I watched. Timothy moaned as he pulled Cara to safety. Soon her feet slipped out and I heard the two of them fall to the ground.

"Thank God! Cara." He exhaled loudly.

I could tell he hugged her.

"I know, I know, let go of me and get Alex out of there." Cara grumbled.

The belt lowered. I wrapped it around my wrist.

"Ready!" I yelled.

Timothy groaned loudly as he pulled me up. I kicked against the sides to try and help him lift me. He grasped me around the shoulders and dragged me on top of him.

We both breathed heavily, face to face. Wisps of my hair fell over my face, but his eyes bore into mine. For the first time I noticed depth to them. They were not a wall, but an inky pool.

"Oh, geez." Cara scoffed at us. "We have to get out of here, people. We don't have time for that touchy-feely junk!"

Timothy rolled me off him and sprang to his feet. I crawled over to kneel by Cara.

"Are you okay?" I asked.

"I feel like I was hit over the head. I'm sure that is going to hang on for a while, but otherwise, yes." She held her forehead and let Timothy prop her up against him.

I insisted on carrying her knapsack. We took a few steps away from the trap.

"Hey, Jared, I think we got something over here!" A gruff voice called out just beyond our sight.

Timothy ducked and pulled Cara onto his back.

"Alex, you are going to have to try and keep up. If you lose me, hide and I will find you." He spoke hurriedly.

Two rugged men rounded the tree next to their trap. "Well, looky here! Hands up where I can see them!" The man yelled. He raised a rifle at us.

Timothy tore off into the woods. I sprinted in the same direction. The rifle fired and I tried running off the trail. Timothy was getting further away.

"Darn it, stop!" One of the men shouted, out of breath from running.

My legs pumped as fast as they could. I could no longer see Timothy. The gun fired again; it was followed by burning in my arm. Blood seeped through a tear in my jacket.

"I think I got her!" One of the men called out. Their footsteps stopped.

I clamped my hand over the wound and searched for a place to hide.

"It won't be hard to find her now. We can just follow the blood."

I walked briskly and I spotted a thicker area of bush. No, that was too obvious. A downed tree stretched across the ground. I climbed over it and squeezed into the space where the tree and the ground met. Quickly I pulled leaves and branches over the exposed part of me.

The men lumbered near. I held my breath and waited for them to pass or find me.

"I don't see any blood. You must not have got her good," the voice said.

"Shoot! I didn't see you take no shots", the man spit.

"That's cause I don't like my gals all marked up." One man jeered.

My skin crawled.

They were almost to the tree now. The pain in my arm had become more of a throb and the blood slipped through my fingers. I felt a little dizzy; it would help if I could get my heart rate down.

The men stopped on the other side of the log. "Come out, come out wherever you are!" One of them laughed. "Peek-a-boo, I see you!" He peered over the log and looked down at me.

One of the men screamed. The man disappeared. A gurgling noise followed. Then the sound of two bodies hit the ground.

I sprang from my hiding spot and began to run. Timothy was instantly wrapped around me. He yanked me to a halt.

I swiped at him. "You left me!"

My left hand slapped bloody prints on his chest. Tears betrayed me and sprang from my eyes.

"Timothy, you left me!"

“You’re hurt.” He pulled me into him. “I’m sorry, Alex, I’m so sorry.”

I sank in to the embrace and allowed myself to cry.

Timothy scooped me up and ran. This time, he held me like a child, careful not to jar me. I rested my head on his chest and tried to stop crying. We didn’t go very far before he shifted me to one arm and climbed a tree. His strength amazed me.

Once in the tree, I saw Cara leaned against the trunk; her legs straddled a thick bough. She looked pale.

“What a freaking mess we are, huh? She’s hurt, too?” She asked weakly.

“Yeah, she got shot, Cara.” Timothy replied.

He sat me on a branch near Cara. I shifted my weight against the trunk.

“She still got my pack?” Cara asked.

“Yeah somehow.” Timothy untangled it from me.

“Everything you need to fix us up is in there.” Cara laid her head back.

Timothy placed a few bottles between his legs. Cara held her hand out for him to pass her one. She opened the bottle and drank. We both watched her, waiting for something to happen.

Timothy turned his attention back to me. "It will take a few minutes, but she will be alright. Thank you for what you did back there." He smiled at me.

I tried to smile back through the pain.

He carefully pulled the jacket from me. He tore the sleeve off my shirt to see the wound better. I bit my bottom lip. The wound left my flesh jagged and blood poured from the hole.

"The good news is you aren't going to die. It's just a flesh wound, but it is deep. I can fix you up but it's going to hurt a little." He said sympathetically.

I thought I saw a grin on Cara's face from the corner of my eye. I shot her a look but the smile was gone. Her eyes were closed and her head tilted back.

Timothy busied himself and poured some of the liquids together. He pulled Cara's knife from his pocket. Blood covered the blade.

"Did you?" I started.

"I had to." He wiped the blood on his pants. He used the knife to mix the solution.

"That doesn't seem too sterile." I commented.

"Trust me, this stuff kills any germs."

He scooped some out with the knife and motioned for me to move my hand from my hurt arm. He spread the mixture over the gash.

"The hardest part is not screaming from the pain." Timothy handed me his belt. "You might want to bite down on this."

I took the belt and immediately the pain spiked. Timothy pulled me into his chest for another embrace, this time to steady me. The wound sizzled and smoked. I clenched my teeth down on the leather. My eyes rolled back in my head. Searing agony spread from the hole in my arm. A moan escaped my mouth and my body shook against Timothy. Then the pain was gone and I went slack. Timothy rested me back against the tree trunk. I looked down at my arm and only a scar of burnt flesh remained.

He moved over to Cara.

She smiled at him. "I knew I wasn't going to get a bath tonight."

He chuckled and looked her over.

"I feel much better, really." Cara snorted.

My eyes felt heavy.

Timothy muttered into Cara's ear. "You know you owe her a thank you. She saved you when I couldn't."

Cara groaned. "Maybe she isn't all that bad, I guess."

Chapter Eight

When I woke it was much later in the day. The sun cast long shadows between the trees. My arm wasn't even sore to the touch. I tested it by rotating it; good as new.

Cara snored softly from her perch. I watched her while she slept. She was pretty in a fairy-type of way. For someone so petite, she was sharp and strong willed. She also had Timothy. I hadn't quite figured out their relationship. I felt weak and alone.

Timothy climbed up the tree. He sat next to me, opening a cloth filled with berries. He offered them to me. We ate in silence and listened to Cara sleep next to us.

"What was that stuff you put on my arm?" I whispered.

"They have that kind of stuff under the ground." He shrugged. "They are far more advanced than humans, in some ways."

"Did the drink you gave Cara work?" I asked.

"It always does." Timothy chuckled. "Saving people is a dangerous business. This ain't our first rodeo."

"I can see that." A smile spread across my face.

"Wow! Is that a smile I see?" Timothy nudged me.

I laughed.

Cara yawned and stretched. "You guys planning on sharing those berries, or what?

I passed a handful to her. She popped the whole thing in her mouth. She moaned, "Those are amazing right now, I'm so hungry".

Timothy handed her more. We all ate in ecstasy as we chewed the juicy berries. They were delicious in our parched mouths.

"If you ladies are up for it, we have another hour of sunlight left. We could still try to make it to the camp." Timothy urged us.

"I'm in." I replied.

"Let's do this." Cara stood uneasily.

"Are you two sure?" Timothy raised an eyebrow at her.

"Yes, but maybe with a little help at first." She reached for his hand.

We made our way down the tree slowly. It felt good to be back on the ground. Even though, I now knew there were more secrets beneath it than the Roars.

We treaded softly among the twigs and leaves. Frost started to take hold of everything. I saw it on my jacket and heard it beneath my feet. I quietly wished for warmer weather soon.

"Timothy?" I crawled over another fallen tree, "What month is it?"

"I believe it is February. It's easy to lose track of time out here." He kept going. "I think we were looking for you for about a month before we found you."

"Are there other compounds like mine?" I wasn't sure I wanted to know.

"Many." Cara interjected.

She looked back to see my face. It must've disappointed her because she went back to watch where she stepped.

"Yes, there are many, probably across the Earth. Different places made for different things." He trailed off.

"What kinds of things?" I didn't look up.

"There are energy sites like the one you were at. Please don't ask about that, yet." He looked back at me and I nodded. “There are all kinds of infrastructure being put in place, some to build for them and some to get rid of what was left by people. There are also places where people are made to hunt down what is left of humans.”

“Wait.” I planted my feet. “You aren’t just taking me back to them, are you, for some type of reward or something?”

Cara faced me. “Sweetheart, they would kill us on sight.”

“Again, Cara is right, and I’m in the business of living.” He never lifted his head.

I believed them; otherwise, they could have already turned me back in. Why walk all this way and go through all the trouble to do that?

“They have spread some rumor that they will pay for people that go missing. It is a lie; they take everyone that shows up. They want everyone left on the outside.” He growled.

“Why do you do this, then? Why save people?”

“It’s more the benefit of having things than it is the saving part.” Cara pointed out.

“Yes, having some place and some things to call my own is nice, but it really is the freedom of choice and being able to live my life the way I want.” Timothy rubbed a mark on the back of his hand.

Cara laughed at his reply.

I hadn't taken notice of the scar before. The way he touched it made me think it had something to do with why he valued freedom. Apparently Cara didn't feel the same.

Soon after our talk, we came to the edge of a clearing. Timothy held his hand out to stop me. The grass grew tall in the meadow, but the bushes and thicket I was used to picking through was absent.

I stood behind the two of them.

Chapter Nine

"You two hide behind a thick tree and let me do the talking." Timothy ordered.

Cara grabbed my arm and pulled me behind the nearest base of a tree. "Keep quiet until he signals us." She drew her knife.

We both peered from the sides of the tree. Timothy raised his hands and took a step into the clearing. Nothing happened. He took another step. I felt sweat trickle down the small of my back.

"Halt!" An ominous voice bellowed. "Who are you and what do you want?"

Timothy didn't waiver. "I only seek a place to stay the night with my travel companions. I am Timothy, the fetcher. I know Elijah; you may ask him."

A few moments passed in silence. I hoped Timothy had a good reputation with this, Elijah.

"How many are there?" The voice called.

Timothy shouted. "Three of us, together, me, and two girls."

There was a pause again as if the message was being sent and answered on the other end. "Let them be seen."

Timothy waved to us without turning around. We slowly crept from our hiding spot and stood next to him. All our hands were raised. I couldn't make out where the voice had come from across the clearing. There was no sign of guards.

"Your entrance has been granted." A voice boomed at us.

We all looked at each other. Timothy walked in between Cara and me. He grabbed both of our hands. "Stay close until we are inside."

We walked across the field and into the shadows of the tree line. It had to be nearing dark now. A guard was waiting for us. He eyed each of us, analyzing, and then turned and marched us to a tall wooden fence. The fence was made with lumber, capped with spikes.

It was hard to believe a fence that stretched that far was invisible across the clearing. It reached wide and tall. There were guards posted every thirty feet or so on platforms. Each bearing a rifle, slung over their backs. Several of the closest guards had their weapons pointed at us.

Our escort directed us to a place in the wall that opened. The gate opened and my senses were immediately bombarded. There were more people inside than I had imagined. They were walking to and from huts carrying pails, food, weapons, or lumber. The people were dressed in layered clothing from before the end of the world, a blur of mismatched colors. Smells filled the air, fire, food, animals, and people, mixed. The sounds of people overwhelmed my brain.

It was almost too much for me. I took a step back and dropped Timothy's hand. There was too much to process. As soon as I digested the scene in one area, it changed. I stood still.

Timothy gently took my hand again and whispered in my ear. "Amazing, isn't it?"

He looked at me as if he understood what I was feeling. After being locked in that prison for the past few years, this was more than amazing. This was pure sensory overload.

The guard called back to us. "Elijah requires that you see him before settling in."

The three of us followed him.

Close by, there was a house that was quite large. In comparison to the other structures, the building was a mansion; the only similarity to the others was a thatched roof. The structure was made from logs instead of boards. Smoke puffed from the stone chimney.

The guard knocked on the door. “The visitors are here!” He announced.

“Send them in!” a voice called from inside.

The guard opened the door and stepped back. “Please go in”.

The three of us entered. The main room was warm from a fire. An elderly man sat in an armchair next to the fireplace. He had a blanket wrapped around his legs.

The man outstretched his arms. “Timothy! Cara! I am so pleased to see you again.”

They both bent and hugged him. He awed over them. He asked about their adventures and checked them over. Cara and Timothy asked him about the village; if there had been any changes since their last visit. They chatted easily, even Cara acted pleasant.

I stood awkwardly and waited for an introduction. Timothy finally took my arm and presented me to Elijah.

“Elijah, this is Alex. She is our newest member of the outside world.”

Elijah waved at me to come closer. I moved to stand at his feet. The old man looked me up and down before he cracked a grin.

“Welcome, I can’t imagine what you have been through at the hands of those animals. I am glad you are safe now. The new world needs as many pretty ladies as it can get. Right, Timothy?”

I looked at Timothy. He was blushed and grinned from ear-to-ear. "It certainly doesn't hurt, old man."

I could feel the blood rush to my cheeks. Cara shot me a look out of the corner of her eye. I pulled nervously at the bottom of my jacket.

"You might as well get used to the extra attention young lady. Not many young ladies made it through the end." Elijah sat forward.

I wasn't sure if I liked him or not. He had a grandfatherly air, but the way he talked about my looks made me uncomfortable. I just smiled so as not to offend him. He obviously had some authority here.

"Timothy, how long do you expect to stay this time?" Elijah asked. He began coughing and spit into a handkerchief.

"Only tonight; we really need a good night's rest." He said.

"I am looking forward to a good wash, too." Cara jumped in.

"Help yourselves. I assume that the same type of lodge works? Same size, same price." He clapped his hands and a teenage boy in rags materialized. "Chris, please take the payment from the nice man."

Timothy dug in Cara's pack and produced a few pieces of gold jewelry. He handed them to the servant boy. Chris scampered away without a word.

I was a little surprised by the exchange. The initial greeting seemed friendly, but everything turned business quickly.

Timothy promised to stop by before we left tomorrow and then he ushered Cara and me out the door. I walked in step with the other two. People were huddled around fires to cook. A loose dog trotted past us. This place was alive.

Cara slapped Timothy's arm. "As good as that bath sounds I have a few things I got to pick up while I'm here."

He turned to me and draped an arm over my shoulder. "It is probably a good idea for you to stick close to me. Elijah took a liking to you and that means the word will spread that there is a new, pretty girl in the village. Some guys like to prey on newborn girls like you."

"Great! That is what people like me are called, newborn? Not to mention the men part gives me the creeps." I watched my feet.

"I know, but wait till you sleep in a real bed again. It will make all those creeps worth it." He teased.

"I have questions now." I looked at his face.

"Ok, shoot." He was calm.

"What is Elijah to this place?" I ventured.

"He is like the mayor or an innkeeper. He makes sure that everything runs and money is made for the village to stay running." Timothy explained.

"What about the servant, Chris?" I went on.

"He is an orphan. Elijah makes sure he is taken care of. It might not look great, but the kid has his needs met and he isn't alone in the world. He would die on his own."

I nodded, but still wondered if that was better than being a slave to Elijah. I had been a slave and I had felt like I died inside. It was slow and I had forgotten what it was like to be alive. I still tried to remember.

We made our way through a maze of people trying to barter goods. Everything from livestock to produce was shoved in our faces. There were women of questionable morals that advertised themselves in little clothing. Men sat around barrels on wooden stools and drank some type of alcohol. I was sure of the alcohol, because of their boisterous and animated demeanors.

I allowed Timothy to pull me into his side. It felt safer to be as close to him as I could get. A few men stared at me in a way that made me uneasy. One yelled an obscene cat-call at me. Timothy raised his head to make sure the man saw his eyes. The man shut up.

Timothy guided me to a small shelter. He held the door for me. I was a little nervous to be alone with him. He had been kind and empathetic, but I also had to remember I was a meal ticket for Cara and him.

Chapter Ten

The whole shack consisted of two rooms. The first room was a sitting room with a couple of wooden chairs and an old scavenged couch. There was a large metal tub near a lit fireplace at the far end of the room. I collapsed onto the couch. It felt so good to sit on something soft.

Timothy disappeared into the back room to check it out. Upon his return, he announced that there were only two beds. He pursed his lips. "I forgot to ask for a place with three beds".

"I will be fine right here." I sighed. "Compared to what I have been sleeping on the last couple of years, I'll take it."

He took a seat across from me. "Are you sure? I don't feel like that is the gentlemanly thing to do."

I giggled. "Don't worry, you have been chivalrous enough."

"Ok, but then you get first dibs on the bath." He stood. "I'll go find someone to fill the tub for you."

"Mmmm. Deal," I muttered.

Timothy laughed at me and left. I pulled off my boots and laid flat on the couch. I didn't even care that it smelled a little musty. The light from the one window in the room caught dust particles in a way that looked like glitter. The outside business was muffled through the walls. My eyes felt heavy.

Timothy returned with clean linens and a young girl that carried two large pails. She was thin and hardened from exposure. Her rags and submissive disposition gave away that she was a servant. My heart sank at the thought.

Timothy placed the linens on the hearth. He introduced us. "Alex, this is Mira; she is going to make you a lovely warm bath."

"That sounds wonderful." I sat up and waited to be told what to do next.

Mira poured the steamy water into the metal tub. "Ma'am, I'll be right back with more water and some soap for you." She bowed in my direction and was gone.

I raised an eyebrow at Timothy. "I'm not sure how I feel about the whole servant situation." I confessed.

"Do you wish to not bathe in protest?" He smirked.

"Try and stand in my way." I tried to sound bold, but I wanted him to get out of my way. I had no intention of exposing myself in front of him, even if it was harmless.

"I am going to go find us some food. Cara might be back before me, let her know." He backed out of the door. "Oh, wrap in a sheet on the hearth. I arranged for someone to wash our clothes."

"Timothy, you are my hero." I joked.

Mira shuffled back in the room with more hot water. She pulled a bar of soap from her apron and placed it by the linens.

"I will leave you to it." She nodded. "Be back in a while to change the water." She gave me a strange look.

"Thank you." I cooed.

It felt so good to be in a place like this. I stood and began to pull off my clothes. The heat of the water stung, but it also soothed my cold bones. My leg ached and I inspected my scar. It had a way of reminding me it was there.

I sank down into the water slowly. I moaned the whole way. I couldn't have imagined a better feeling in the world. The sounds from the village could still be heard through the walls to remind me that I wasn't completely alone.

I scrubbed years of grime from my skin. We were only allowed sponge baths in the camp. My hair and scalp stripped of the soil and sweat. I was me again, well, as close as I could get to the old me.

Cara barged in the front door. I sloshed around making sure I was covered. She shut the door and gave me a frown. “Aw man, you beat me to it.” She whined.

“It’s ok, Timothy is having the girl switch out the water for each of us.” I offered.

“He is such a good man, eh?” She joked, but stopped quickly. “Speaking of, where is that bugger?”

I nodded, with the towel wrapped around myself modestly. “He went to find us food.”

“The man is a genius." She giggled. “I’ll grab the linen for you.”

She plopped her full knapsack to the floor. Cara retrieved a bleached white sheet from the hearth and stretched it open.

She turned her head. “I won’t look. Good grief, you better hurry before Timothy gets back if you are that worried about anyone seeing you in there.”

I quickly got out and wrapped myself in the sheet. The water was a muddy brown, which didn’t surprise me. Cara dragged a chair over to the fireplace for me. She was being uncharacteristically thoughtful.

"Thank you." I smiled and basked in the heat of the fire.

"So, what's the sleeping situation?" Cara walked into the other room.

"No worries, I called the couch." I stated.

I heard her throw herself onto one of the beds. She groaned loudly. I smiled; it felt good to not be the only one excited about the little things.

Mira came back and began to prepare the tub for Cara. Cara wasn't as bashful about the bath.

She stripped and got in instantly. She didn't seem at all fazed by us in the room.

Mira kept her head down and avoided Cara. I found it odd that she didn't acknowledge Cara. I decided it was about time to start asking some of the tough questions. Maybe I would talk to Timothy after dinner.

Timothy looked so proud of himself. He returned with smoked chicken, corn on the cob, and leaven bread. Cara waved us into the other room to eat so she could bathe. We sat on the beds and inhaled the food. Both of us grunted and moaned while we savored it.

"Thank you." I stopped to lick my fingers. "For all of this."

"Alex, we all needed this. A little civilization in our lives to remind us why we are running."

Timothy grinned. He tore some meat from the bone.

"I think it is time for me to know." I felt like I was invading by asking.

"I know. The guy in the market and Mira kind of brought the issue back up, huh?" He stared at his food.

"Kind of." I replied. "It's easy to forget that you aren't like me but then you do something that a normal person couldn't. Like, carry me running through the forest faster than anything I've seen."

"I will take that as a compliment. It took some time to adapt to your ways." He picked at the chicken bone. He slowly answered. "We come from them, under the earth."

Chapter Eleven

I had known deep down, but the confirmation shocked me. The thought was different from reality. I looked up at him and he met my gaze. He looked me over. I think he waited for a scream, or for me to run, or pass out, or something.

I swallowed. "Okay, how?" It was all I managed.

"Cara and I were part of a colony under the earth. It is further down than any of you can drill or tunnel. Our people had been planning to come to the surface for some time. Your people had to know there was something going on down there. For instance, the frequent earthquakes and tidal waves; they were from our explosives, expanding in areas closer to the surface." He lay back on the bed.

I nodded. It did make sense. In the years before the first real Roar earthquakes and tidal waves had occurred more and more often. Many people died from what we believed were natural disasters.

He went on. "We had been taught to believe that one day the Earth would be ours. From birth, we were indoctrinated to believe that the people on the surface would kill the Earth. Unfortunately, your people lived up to that. We were made to watch scenes of your wars, famine, pollution, and all other human evil. It was a form of brainwashing."

My head sank even further. I couldn't look at him. As a race we had messed up. We fought over a million things, land, resources, religion, and many even pettier reasons. We allowed people to starve to death. I remembered children on television that were starved with their bellies distended.

Many of our oceans were over fished. People had screwed up and there had been oil flowed into our greatest resource. I even recalled a visit to a beach where I had carried grocery bags to pick up trash left by other people during the day, filling them over and over. We had slowly killed the planet we inhabited.

"I understand that." I agreed. "But your people killed us for our mistakes and they are using us as slaves!"

"I know." Timothy looked at me. "Some of us found out about that. A few of my people played a video cast of the initial Roar. I couldn't allow that to happen to a whole race of people. It was sickening to think we did that. I knew the scale of what we did immediately. That's when I met Cara. She had worked along healers and often carried correspondence for them. She found me in our colony. Cara had been looking at her messages and knew a lot more about the plans for your people than I did."

Cara entered the room wrapped in her sheet. "We were part of a regimented life. I knew something wasn't right. I guess my moral compass took over." She sat on the bed next to me.

Timothy smiled at her. "It wasn't right. Long story short, we decided to defect and leave it all behind." He reassured me.

"The best way we could help and survive was this." Cara pointed at me.

"So, all of this is so your kind can live on the surface?" I asked.

Timothy answered. "Yes, they truly believe that to save our world, they have to."

"The solution was to kill billions of people?" I was disgusted.

Cara looked at me right in my eyes. "Alex, you know the Earth can't go on the way it is. However, the way they are going about it is wrong."

Cara put her hand on mine. I wanted to pull mine away, but it felt good to be touched.

"So, you are running from them too? You defected?" I probed.

"Yes, if we end up back with them, they will kill us." Cara admitted. She looked at her lap.

"We are the most hated of our kind. They can't control us with the Roar. We know their technology and healing recipes. That is how we rescued you. We knew that they were going to have you stay late. It gave Timothy an opportunity to speak to you alone."

I looked at her in amazement. I sat beside someone that had not seen the light of day as they grew up.

Again, they confirmed my belief that they were not like me. I had heard their story and they had given me the chance to form my own opinion of them.

Cara rubbed my hand and spoke softly. "Why don't you rest? I think that is enough for today."

I got up and staggered to the couch. My eyes fluttered while Mira readied the bath for Timothy. She moved mechanically about the room. I wanted to ask her about the others. How had she survived? How had she become a bath maid?

Instead, I rolled over on the couch, my nose against the cushions. The sun had disappeared below the horizon a long time ago. I heard Timothy fumble with his clothes. Then he sunk into the tub. I drifted into sleep.

My dreams took me beneath the Earth. People chipped away and moved the ground inside tunnels. The people looked like us, except their eyes were white. They were completely white, the opposite of Cara's and Timothy's.

A woman walked between the workers and a horn sounded. The people turned and made their way to a large cavern. Enormous screens came to life with images. Most were of landscapes void of people's influence. Mountains hovered in the distance, beaches remained unscathed, and plains spread across golden horizons.

"This is what we work for! This is our Earth! We will no longer be chained by the restraints of dirt and the darkness of our tunnels!" A voice boomed.

An applause erupted and the vision changed view. From above the cavern I saw the immense crowd below. There were more people than there were stars in the sky.

I awoke with a start. Timothy hovered over me.

It was dark and I clutched the sheet to me.

"Sh, it's ok. I just wanted you to go outside with me." He requested.

"What are you doing?" I mumbled. My eyes tried to come into focus.

His eyes weren't black as they were before. They were completely white. It shocked me and I sat back on the couch.

"Wha- what?" I stuttered.

"I wanted you to see me and I want to explain." He held out a hand to me.

Reluctantly, I took his offered hand. His face urged me to follow. He pulled me to the door, a finger over his lips, telling me to stay quiet. Our feet padded on the raised wood.

Outside he sat on the porch and motioned for me to sit next to him. I looked around; there was still noise coming from the market area. The barrels still flowed with ale, I supposed. I sat down.

"I can tell you neither of us have ever had someone we were saving actually save one of us. I really meant it when I thanked you. It was a shock to me that one of you would do that for us."

"I had to Timothy. You two are taking me to my new home." I admitted.

He nodded. "But, I had always rescued weak people. You have no idea how many times I have risked my own life and Cara has risked hers." He shook his head. "I know this is a lot for you to come to terms with, but I am beginning to realize that you are a lot stronger than I expected."

I blurted. "Now, you can begin with why your eyes are white?"

He rubbed his eyes. "I wanted to show you. These are my real eyes. We wear dark tinted contacts most of the time. The sun is too much for us. Coming from generations beneath the Earth we have evolved to this. We can see in the dark but the light blinds us."

I took a deep breath. "This is a lot for me. I just had a dream that your eyes were like that."

A strange look spread across his face and he rubbed the scar on the back of his hand. "I think you are stronger than most of the people we run across. Most are afraid or angered that we come from the people that did this." He explained.

"I get it. I'm just not sure how to feel right now. I am alone is this world until I find out who paid you to come for me." I said harsher than I meant.

Timothy reached for my hand. "Right now, I am glad I was paid to save you."

I stood. "I appreciate that. I have a lot to sort out. You must remember, I lost my family. You don't know the things I have seen."

Timothy bowed his head. "I can only guess."

I went back to the couch. I stared at the tub. Timothy came through the door and went straight to bed. Being woken up had startled me enough that I couldn't go back to sleep. I restlessly dozed off and on for hours.

At some point, our clothes had been brought back. They were stacked in one of the chairs. I retrieved mine and hurriedly dressed. I decided I was going to sneak out. Maybe I could find Mira and get a human perspective of what this world had become. She obviously had seen things by the way she reacted around them.

I jumped off the front porch. My boots made too much noise on the wood. It was near dawn and the village was quiet. I looked up and down the dirt corridor. I walked the way Timothy went to find Mira.

The wind stung my cheeks. Smoke curled from chimneys. The smoke looked like ghosts that rose from each shelter. I wrapped my arms around myself and walked briskly. I looked back before I rounded a corner to make sure I wasn't being followed.

I turned right into a shadowy figure. A hand clamped around my mouth. I could immediately smell that it wasn't Timothy. Alcohol and body odor filled my nose and I heaved. The man had me around the waist and lifted my feet off the ground. I clawed at his arm. He threw me to the ground. It knocked the air out of me. I choked trying to catch my breath. I rolled over to see my attacker for the first time.

He was huge; muscle and fat bulged from different places. He grabbed me by the hair and pulled me up, putting me in a head lock. I writhed and swatted at him, but I had not recovered from being thrown. I couldn't breathe, let alone scream.

My scalp was on fire and he continued to yank me over to a stone wall that lined the path. He shoved me against the rock and pressed himself against me. He crushed the last bit of air from my lungs. One hand squeezed my face. His pock marked face was in mine and bared his rotten teeth.

"I heard we got ourselves a pretty new girl." He hiccupped. "They were right." He spat as he talked. The man licked my face and I dry heaved again. I squirmed against the pressure of him. He laughed.

"That's no way to treat the new pretty girl in town." A voice said evenly. It was Timothy, thank God.

"Mind your own business boy." The man snarled.

"She is my business." Timothy ripped the man from me.

I dropped to my knees. The man staggered off balance, but still swung at Timothy. He dodged the hit and answered with a left hook to the guy's mouth. Blood spurted from his lips on impact and the man collapsed.

Timothy scooped me off the ground. He cradled me in his arms just as he did in the woods.

"Are you ok?" He asked.

I managed a nod.

"That was really stupid Alex. If I hadn't had the dream that woke me, I wouldn't have gone to check on you. Do you understand how bad that could have been if I hadn't heard you leave and followed you?" He was angry now.

"I am so sorry." I cried. Tears ran down my face.

Timothy carried me back to the shack. He laid me on the couch. I was ashamed of myself. To go out at night unarmed and by myself was stupid.

Timothy leaned down and growled. “I don’t even care what you were doing out there.” He pointed to the door. “Promise me that you won’t do something like that again.”

A sob burst from my lips and I nodded. “Thank you.”

“Do I need to sleep in one of these chairs to keep an eye on you?” He put his hands on his hips.

“Oh, Timothy, I didn’t mean to. I wasn’t running away.” I sniffled. “I just wanted to hear about what happened from another person like me. You must realize that I have been a slave to your people for years. I lost my family because of them. Even if you are telling me the truth, I am blindly following strangers that lived among those th-things.”

Timothy straightened and spat back. “I really thought you were different. I thought you saw that we are trying to help you.”

“You are getting paid to deliver me. That is your job. I am a shipment for a well-paid job.” I retorted.

“Sure, you got it all figured out Alex.” He narrowed his eyes as he spoke.

Cara appeared in the doorway. “Can you two keep it down out here? What are you fighting about anyway?” She asked, scratching her stomach.

“Nothing, nothing at all.” Timothy replied. He turned and brushed past Cara to the other room.

"Wow, you got him going good." Cara yawned. I turned my back to her. She groaned and retreated to bed.

I was too angry and embarrassed to sleep. Thank goodness, it wasn't too long before the sun started to rise. My bones ached from trying to stay still. Streams of daylight found their way through the window and curtains.

Soon, the noises of a busy daytime, began in the village. Voices permeated the thin walls. Deals were being made in the street.

There was a loud rap on the door. "Open up!" A voice startled me.

I jumped up and ran into the other room. Both Timothy and Cara were scrambling to get dressed. Timothy looked at me. "It's got to be the guards. That jerk from last night must've filed a fake complaint."

There was another pounding on the door.

"Who? What happened last night?" Cara was exasperated.

"Cara, we don't have time." Timothy wrapped his arm through mine.

"I am so sorry." I apologized. I looked in Timothy's eyes.

"It may be time for you to save my life, now." He said as he swung open the door.

Two guards pushed their way inside. They immediately seized Timothy and tied his hands behind his back.

Cara sprang upon them. "Wait! What did he do?"

"He was reported for attacking a man last night." The guard announced and shoved Timothy toward the door.

"But he didn't, that man was attacking me. Timothy saved me!" I pled. I clung onto his arm.

Cara was shocked. She took a step back. I let go of Timothy and reached for her. She cursed at me and sidestepped out of my reach.

"This is the kind of trouble you will get by running around with these things." The other guard nodded at Cara.

They stumbled out of the door and onto the road. A small crowd had formed to watch the drama. Cara ran around me and blocked their way. It stopped them.

"Where are you taking him? Wait till Elijah hears what you have done to his friend!" She shouted at the guards.

They laughed. "Elijah is the one that ordered the warrant for him."

Timothy kept his mouth closed. His gaze was thoughtful, as he tried to think his way out of this.

Cara looked at him and then at me. She stomped past me into the shack. I watched them march

Timothy away. People in the crowd yelled insults and spit in his direction. I closed my eyes and took a deep breath before I walked back in to deal with Cara.

"You had better tell me what happened, NOW!" She was in a rage.

"I messed up." I raised my hands in surrender.

"No joke! Keep talking." She yelled.

"I woke up during the night. I wanted to talk to another person about what happened when the world ended. A man attacked me in the street." I began to choke up.

Cara sighed. "And Timothy saved you. What did he do to the guy?"

"He punched the guy. He may have knocked out a couple of teeth." I shrugged.

"That doesn't sound too bad. I am going to go talk to Elijah and try to figure this out. He should understand why Timothy hit him. Get our stuff together and wait for me. Do not leave for any reason. Do you understand?"

I put all our stuff in a pile by the door and sat on the couch to wait.

Cara barged in after what felt like forever. She looked down at me on the couch, sympathetically.

"As mad as I am at you for getting us into this mess, I am sorry that I am about to have to ask this of you." She lowered herself to sit on the floor.

I closed my eyes and put my head in my hands. This meant there was bad news.

"The filthy pig that attacked you last night was the perfect excuse for Elijah to take Timothy. That old geezer knows that my people will pay dearly for him. What Elijah is too stupid to realize is if they turn him over to our people, they will disintegrate this place and all the people in it, just to set an example." Cara explained.

"Tell me what I have to do." I interrupted.

Cara breathed out. "Elijah said he would let Timothy go on one condition, we trade you for him. You apparently made quite an impression on the old dirt bag."

"It's my fault." I clasped my hands around my knees.

"Listen." She pulled herself on to the couch beside me. "I have no intention of just leaving you. Timothy and I have a much better chance of rescuing you than you and I have of getting him out of there. I have a plan."

Cara explained the plan. She also told me that she had seen Timothy and in a brief embrace, she told him to follow our lead whenever he saw us again. The plan seemed simple and straightforward, it should work, but it didn't make me feel less nervous.

Cara's people were known in this new world for self-preservation. That was the message I got from the reactions of people and the stories Timothy shared. The idea was to try and roll with that. I hoped that Elijah would buy that the two of them saw me as a meal ticket and that I was disposable. I just truly hoped that wasn't the case. If it was, I was about to be Elijah's property.

At the door to Elijah's house, a guard waited for us. "You must be the two I am waiting for." He grinned at me. "You are certainly worth the old man's time."

My stomach turned. Cara grabbed my arm and shoved me into the main room with a knife at my back. Elijah sat in his chair by the fire. The two guards from earlier stood on either side of Timothy. Timothy's eyes widened at the sight of us. Cara was delivering me as a prisoner. I struggled against Cara's grip on my arm.

"Cara, I always knew you were a sensible girl." Elijah gripped the armrests on his chair.

"No!" I thrashed against her strength.

Timothy winced at my shriek. He couldn't look at me and allow this, so he stared at the floor.

Cara pushed me to the ground. "She's yours Elijah, just let Timothy go. We will be on our way. I don't want any more trouble."

Elijah smiled. "As promised, your brother."

One of the guards kicked Timothy in the back. I looked back at Cara. Timothy was her brother! She helped Timothy to his feet. Somehow, we hadn't even had that conversation.

Timothy looked me over for signs that I was going along with all of this. I was trying to be as convincing, as possible. A couple of years in the camp had made me a professional at acting.

"Thank you for this most fantastic barter. You two will be escorted to the gates. If you ever return, I will personally return you to your people to collect my reward." He waved them out.

"No! Don't leave me here!" I threw myself at Cara's feet.

She kicked me off. "Sorry Alex, it's not personal. It's business."

They left. I screamed at the top of my lungs. A guard materialized from the back room with a rope in one hand and a strip of cloth in the other. He flipped me face down, gagged me, and tied my hands. I kicked and writhed against him.

He lifted me and presented me to Elijah.

Chapter Twelve

"My dear, there is no need for all of that. Here I was going to invite you to have dinner with me, but I can't have such a violent guest at my table." He said calmly. "I think we should give her a little alone time to reflect upon her choices."

The guard threw me over his shoulder and took me out a back door of the house. There was a small stone structure with a wooden door against the house. There was a deadbolt on the outside of the door. I hadn't noticed Chris, Elijah's servant, followed us. The guard tossed me flat on to the ground. I tried to catch my breath.

Chris knelt beside me and whispered. "You had better do what is asked. If Elijah likes you, you might be treated well." He smoothed my hair. "If you displease him, there are many ways for him to punish you."

Chris stood and slapped the guard. I was shocked when the guard didn't react.

"This is one that displeased Elijah. Show her what happens when Elijah is not happy." He hit the guard with a stick in the back.

The guard leaned over me and opened his mouth.

There was no tongue, only a nub at the back of his throat. I squirmed away. Maybe this plan had all been a big mistake.

Chris laughed. "I would strongly suggest that you get yourself under control so that when we come back we will be able to get you cleaned up and presentable for Elijah." He kicked me in the stomach.

I curled into a ball and coughed into my gag.

"Elijah demands that you do not hit her. He doesn't want her all marked up on that pretty face of hers. You will guard her." Chris demanded of the guard, turned on his heels and disappeared.

The guard opened the small door and pushed me through. There was barely enough room to sit upright. The door closed behind me. I watched the shadows of the guard through the slats in the rickety door.

The silence was a curse. I had too much to think about. I was now in the hands of Elijah, a patriarch in this village. No one here was going to save me. I had to have hope, something I had shut off from my life before. I had to hope that Timothy and Cara would come back for me.

The plan did make sense. The two of them were much more equipped to come back for me instead of Cara and me taking on the task of saving Timothy.

Fear ran through me, nonetheless. I had no idea when or truly, if they would come back for me. I had to hope that the people in this place had them all wrong. It scared me that Elijah had known them longer than me and counted on them giving me up so easily.

I kicked at the dirt. I wondered if Timothy had been kept in here during his capture. Maybe he had sat here and wondered if we would come for him.

Time passed at a painful pace. I kept track as I watched the angle of the sun as it came through the cracks in the door. Eventually, dusk came and there was little light in my cell at all.

Shadows moved outside closer to the door. It cracked open and Chris squatted in the doorway.

"Are you ready to play nice?" He reached in and took a handful of my hair.

I nodded and scooted forward.

"Good girl, I am going to let you crawl out of there. Then, we will get you all fixed up for dinner, if you are a good girl. If you try anything, I have this." He pulled a knife from his belt. "But we don't want to play that game, do we?"

I shook my head and clumsily emerged from the cell. He had to help me to my feet. It took a minute for me to get my stance and bearings.

Chris poked me in the back. "We will be going into the house and heading straight to the bathing room. You look a mess." He turned to the guard still sitting opposite of the doorway. "Doesn't she?"

The guard groaned at us and found his feet. He came up behind the two of us. I followed Chris into a section of the house you couldn't tell existed from the outside. Down steep stairs, we entered the basement.

Mira and another girl were busy making the room look more formal than needed. I am sure I looked shocked to see her there.

The floor was tiled with flat stone, as were the walls. It was extremely cold below the house despite another lit fireplace. A large free-standing tub sat in front of the fire. Steam rose from the water.

Mira wiped her hands on her apron. "Fancy to see you, again." She smiled.

"Trust me, this wasn't by choice." I said in a low voice.

"People don't usually find themselves down here any other way." She clapped her hands and the other girl stopped and faced me. "This is Sadie, she is my new assistant." Mira said pleasantly.

Sadie bowed.

"I acquired her after a recent promotion to Elijah's home." A smirk spread across her face.

I had a distinct feeling that I was here by her doing. Among four captors, I could only use my stare as a threat.

"Do what you can to make her presentable." Chris directed. "You have an hour before Elijah expects her at dinner."

Chris started to climb the stairs. He spoke to the guard. "Give the girls a little privacy; you may wait at the top of the stairs."

The mute left us to the task at hand.

Mira gave me a once over and poked me. "An hour, huh, I guess we will make it work."

"Amazing how some people grow a little sassy when they aren't working the slums anymore." I pointed out.

"You are lucky Elijah doesn't like his ladies marked up, because that would earn you a slap in the face. Be careful." She warned. "Undress."

I stripped my now dirtied uniform to the floor. Sadie came to help me into the tub. I was incredibly aware of my naked body in front of two strangers.

"Scrub her down and wring her hair, we need it to dry quickly," Mira instructed Sadie. "I'll be back in a moment. I need to bring the dress down."

Sadie took the bar of soap and roughly lathered my hair. I decided that no matter how much it hurt, I wouldn't let her see.

She worked the soap through my hair. Sadie then poured a pitcher of scalding water on my head. I grit my teeth.

"Alex, is that what they call you?" Sadie asked once the footsteps on the stairs stopped.

I answered with silence. She yanked a brush through my wet hair. I felt small clumps being pulled from my scalp.

"You know, I can make this more pleasant for you, if you will talk to me." She said primly and dropped a wad of hair into the tub. "It gets so boring taking orders all the time. So, I'll ask again, is your name Alex?"

I nodded this time.

Sadie patted my back and used a cloth to wash my back. "Isn't that better?"

I nodded again.

"I do feel sorry for you. I can't imagine being kidnapped by those monsters." She whispered sympathetically.

"It seems like we have very different opinions about what is considered a monster." I sneered.

"We hear all kinds of stories about them. Many say they eat humans, is that true?" She paused.

"I don't think all of them do. For the most part, they have been kind to me. Timothy even saved me a couple of times."

Sadie gasped and moved a stool to my side. She frowned. "My Ma told me they are taking everything they can from us so they can get rid of us all."

"I can't believe they are all like that. I think some of them don't want to do that." As I talked, I realized that I meant it. I wanted it to be true.

Sadie handed me the cloth. "I'll let you keep some of your decency."

"Thank you." I took the cloth and cleaned myself.

"Mira will be back any minute." Sadie hurried. She pointed at my leg, "How did you get that?" She meant my scar.

"I don't remember." I said truthfully.

She shrugged. "Hopefully, the dress will hide it. I do wish you luck. Elijah can be odd and the fact that he took a liking to you could be either good or bad."

"I know, I saw the guard that made him mad." I admitted.

She nodded. "Honey, that isn't the worst I've seen."

I took a deep breath. "Then, I guess I better not make him mad."

The stairs creaked, which announced Mira's arrival. She swept in to the bathing room and carried a gaudy long gown covered in sequins. I quickly noticed the high slit up one side and the low-cut neck line. My heart stopped. Thank goodness, the slit was on the opposite leg as my scar. The low neckline proposed that I might be entertaining more than dinner.

"Isn't this dress to die for?" Mira sang. Sadie nodded and blushed.

"I am so jealous." She held it to her and danced across the room.

"By all means Mira, you are welcome to take my place." I crinkled my nose at her.

She came close and hissed. "Too bad it does have one flaw." She held the dress in front of me. She pointed to the little hole. "Do you see it? It is where Elijah had his last dinner date stabbed for being a dull companion."

I tried to look unfazed. What kind of sicko was I dealing with here?

"Get her out." Mira ordered and went back to dancing with the dress.

Sadie helped me up and out into a towel. She directed me to a chair where she worked to style my hair up. When she was finally happy with the result, I was given to Mira.

Mira held the dress so that I could step in to it. She lifted the straps over my shoulders. The dress was twisted into place on my body. The sequins scratched my skin. I had yet to feel so out of place in this world.

Mira whistled at me. "I do think that you will make Elijah happy."

Then she started to zip the dress. Somewhere around my hips, she began to tug.

"Oops, maybe I spoke too soon. You are going to have to suck in." She slapped my behind.

I sucked in as much as possible. Sadie pushed on my front to help. The dress slowly began to zip. It was tight, but it zipped all the way. I could feel the fray of the small hole under my breast. It made me shiver in disgust.

Both Mira and Sadie gawked at me.

"You look beautiful." Sadie squeaked.

Mira struck Sadie across the face. "Shut up."

Sadie held her cheek and went to cleaning up the room. She didn't speak again.

"It is time for me to present you to your new master." Mira jeered.

She took my hand and we climbed the stairs. On the way, I tried to focus and swallow the fear creeping up my throat. I had expected Timothy and Cara to have come back by now. I prayed that nothing had happened and that I just needed to wait it out. I hoped they wouldn't be too late.

At the top of the stairs, I reminded myself that I was good at acting. The time I had been spent digging for the invisible masters had prepared me for hiding my true feelings. I could do what was needed to survive, but I knew even I had limits.

Mira pushed me in front of her. Chris and the mute guard waited for us.

"My lord, Mira!" Chris exclaimed. "I do think this will make Elijah very happy. You can expect to become our new hand maiden on a more permanent basis."

She beamed at him. "I would be honored." She curtsied and passed me off. She turned and disappeared down to the basement.

I held my head high. The guard winked at me. Chris held his arm out for mine. We walked to the dining hall.

Chapter Thirteen

Chris unlocked a chain wrapped between two large wooden doors. I pushed down the fear that came with the idea of being locked in a room with Elijah.

"It's for security. We don't want your little friends intruding if they decide to come back for any reason." Chris smirked.

As he opened the door I whispered. "You know, I felt sorry for you. I couldn't believe this world had gone back to slavery among humans."

He opened his mouth, but closed it when he saw Elijah standing a few feet away to greet us. I had timed my jab just right. I smiled at Elijah.

I kept my eyes forward. Elijah took a step back and leaned against a chair.

"You are more beautiful than I could have imagined." He said in awe.

The table in the center of the room was dark wood, polished richly. Only two high backed chairs sat at the table. Both adorned with red velvet cushions. There was a massive candelabra sitting on the table which lit the room. I quickly noticed that the door we came through was the only entrance and there were no windows. My heart sank.

I steadied myself. “Thank you.”

“Well, stop standing there and help the lady to her seat.” He waved to Chris.

Chris pulled back one of the chairs for me. I felt the cold stone floor under my bare feet. I sat carefully as to not stretch the dress beyond its ability.

Elijah eyes never left me. That made me very uncomfortable.

“You two can ask the help to bring dinner. We will eat alone. You may lock the door as soon as dinner is served.” Elijah instructed.

Chris bowed slightly and rushed the guard from the room. Chris swatted at the guard to make him move faster.

A moment later, Mira and Sadie entered the room with stemware and carafes. They paused and looked at each other to pour in unison, which seemed to please Elijah. He smiled at me. The red wine looked like blood in my glass, it made my stomach curl. I almost expected the liquid to coagulate in the bottom of the glass.

I wondered what Mira would think about being called, “the help.” I put that away for use later. The thought lifted my spirits a little.

The girls marched from the room and returned a second later with silver dishes piled high. Mira served me the platter of greens, dark meat, mushrooms, and a chunk of bread. The smells made my mouth water and I swallowed to keep from drooling over it.

Everyone’s actions seemed so rehearsed. I felt as though we were all on a stage for Elijah. Our main goal was to entertain him.

“May I please have some water, too?” I asked. My voice was sweet.

Mira looked to Elijah for an answer.

“Of course, my dear, but I do highly recommend the wine. I do wish for you to enjoy it.” I took that as a demand for me to drink the wine during dinner. \

I smiled primly. “Yes Sir, I am sure it is lovely.”

Mira brought me another glass filled with water. It had been too long since I drank and I knew the water was a necessity. My mouth had gone dry as soon as we had entered the dining room.

Mira came beside me to place the water on the table. I couldn't resist the opportunity with her so close to me. I ground my heel into her bare toes. She flinched, cursed at me, and spilled some of the water on the table.

I caught the glass to save it from shattering on the floor. I tried to look shocked at Mira's foul language and held the napkin to my mouth.

Elijah raged, "How dare you, you clumsy cow! Guard, remove her at once!"

The mute guard sprang into the room. For a split second, I wasn't sure whom he was ordering to leave.

Then Mira dropped to her knees. "Please, please my lord. Don't do this, it was an accident."

"This is unacceptable, get rid of her." Elijah forced himself to stand. His face was red with anger.

Guilt caused me to interject. "It was my fault." All eyes turned to me. "It was my foot that made her trip. Please have mercy on her."

Elijah stared at me and then relented. "Please leave," was all he said. Both Mira and the guard exited; the doors shut behind them. I could hear the chain and lock latched from the outside.

"I am sorry for that." Elijah shook his head. "It is so hard to find good help."

"It's ok, Mira didn't mean too, I am sure." My voice wavered.

"Please, don't make excuses for the help." Elijah nodded at me. "We will have a wonderful time despite her. Please eat."

I picked up the fork. The food looked so good, I wanted to inhale it, but I resisted, it could be poisoned.

"I do apologize for having to be so inhospitable to you earlier, but see, it has greatly changed your outlook on things." He took a bite of the greens. "I assure you, the food is safe. I intend on keeping you around for a while. I grow so lonely here." He chewed loudly.

I made the decision to play the game. Say what is expected and do what I needed to do to buy Cara and Timothy more time. I took a bite as well. It was heavenly.

"Is it really so lonely?" I shrugged. "You run this village. People are willing to tend to your every want. You must be very well liked by your people."

Elijah laughed. "Yes, I am very well liked because I rule with an iron fist!" He slammed his hand on the table.

I jumped and forced myself to giggle. "So, it seems. Please tell me the story of how you came to rule this place with an iron fist."

My mother taught me that trick. Most people would talk for hours about themselves if given the chance.

Elijah settled in to tell me his story. I ate and nodded when obligated, but listened also. I may learn something that could prove useful at another time. He told me about his old life. He had always maintained a bachelor status, even as an aging man. I gathered that he thought women were the inferior sex, shallow, and less intelligent.

Elijah did mention a son that probably died during the first Roar. That spurred his hatred of the "moles" as he called them. He had survived by chance. As a retired professor, much of his time was spent fishing. The lake had saved him from the fate many found.

Afterwards, people lost their minds and killed each other for supplies or starved. Many people couldn't survive in this new world without medicine, direction, or know how. Our society had become too dependent on technology and reverted to survival of the fittest.

A small group of people had started to form out here in the woods. They lived in chaos. When he came, they were desperate for someone to lead them. Elijah's story made him a hero of kingly status.

People from all over came when they heard of the civilization that had been built. It was very clear that Elijah thought highly of himself.

Something had been bothering me about the fact that so many people could live here and the "moles" as he called them had not come for them.

I bravely ventured to ask him. "Why have the moles not come for you?"

"Ah, that is the less glamorous side to all of this." He went on. "They do know we are here and we have a delicate arrangement with them. I have only seen a few of them in my time here. One came in the early days as an ambassador to meet with me. A deal was struck and every new moon a few from our village disappears. They are a sacrifice for the rest of us to continue living. Of course, there are some of us off limits, I negotiated that. No one in my home may ever be taken."

"That was very smart of you, but you can't trust them, can you?" I prodded.

He took a sip of wine. "Well, upon negotiations, I was able to learn a few things." His eyes twinkled. "I entertained the mole and made sure to keep the wine flowing. They are intelligent creatures, but alcohol is banned where they come from. It makes the mind weak, they say. In the negotiator's case, they were right."

"What kind of things did he tell you?" I leaned forward, urging him. I fingered the outline of the dress around the low cut.

Elijah sat back in his chair and admired me from across the table. "For one, the largest machines that brought the end of the world are broken. It took all the energy they had stored to produce the largest Roar. Smaller machines are still operational, but they only have the ability to control the camps and surrounding areas. We picked an amazing place to start a village because it happens to be far enough from any of them."

"So, there can't be another large Roar?" I grinned. There was some hope after all. I continued to trace the neckline of the dress.

"I didn't say that, my dear, there could be, but we have some time. They are working on gathering more energy and are working on the machines. I hoped to remain cordial with Timothy, the fetcher, and his sister. They always paid heavily for their keep." He sighed. "I was going to offer them quite an amount for you. Then the mishap occurred last night with that dreadful fellow. Mind you, I am aware of that scoundrel, but to keep the peace in the village, I had to ban your friends. It also gave me an opportunity to make the trade for you."

I chewed my last bite and swallowed. "Well, I do thank you for that. I definitely prefer civilization to running around in the woods." I lied.

He smiled and pushed back his chair. "I am glad you feel that way. Talking with you has pleased me."

Elijah walked over to me. His hands on the high back of my chair. He leaned to my ear and spoke. "I can make sure that you enjoy many comforts in the civilization I have created."

His breath tickled my ear. He traced a finger down my cheek. I held my breath to hide my disgust for him.

There was a small noise above us. Both of us turned our eyes to the ceiling.

I knocked my fork from the table. It clattered on the stone floor loudly.

"I am so sorry." I apologized.

I pushed my chair back in to him and bent down to retrieve it.

He reeled for a moment, which put some space between us. The sound above was louder now. A large sword protruded through the thatching. Elijah looked from me to the sword.

"Guard!" he yelled as he reached for me. I ran around to the other side of the table. "Guard, get in here, now!" Elijah bellowed.

The sword cut a square out of the thatching. Timothy dropped through the hole in the roof.

After gaining his bearings, he ran to me, shoving the old man to the ground. Elijah cried out in pain. The chain on the door rattled.

"Get on my back and hold on tight." Timothy scooped me up.

The door banged open. Timothy jumped on top of the table. He leapt to the rafters, swinging us through the opening. The hole led to a night sky. I looked over my shoulder to see the mute guard gaping at us from below.

"Don't stand there like an idiot! Get them!" Elijah spit.

Timothy navigated to the frame of the roof, skipping over the wooden beams. At the edge of the house, he picked up speed and sprang onto the nearest tree.

I was scared out of my mind. I closed my eyes and wrapped my legs tighter. There was yelling from below. Timothy picked his way around the tree and the large perimeter fence was within reach.

A gun shot rang out. It hit a nearby limb. I muffled a scream by clenching my teeth. Timothy caught the edge of the wall with both hands and slid over. We dropped to the ground.

I rolled off Timothy on impact. He had me in his arms instantly. "Are you ok?"

"I-I think so." I stuttered.

"They will come looking for us; we have to get going. Do you think you can hold on a little longer?" He asked and held me out to looking me over.

I nodded. I had never been so happy to see someone in my life. He draped me over his back again and took off into the dark woods. He moved so fast it hardly felt like we touched the ground

We heard the noises of a search party behind us. Men yelled at one another. Leaves and sticks crackled in the distance.

Another gunshot startled us. I buried my head into Timothy's neck. I trembled with fear, even though I knew there was no way they could keep up with Timothy's speed.

Chapter Fourteen

Finally, he slowed down. He turned his head to listen. We had to be at least two miles from Elijah's village. It was then I realized I had torn the dress badly. To wrap myself around Timothy the slit had ripped up to my hip. The cold air made me shiver.

Timothy, felt me shake. "Of course, that dirty old man would put you in the least clothes possible."

He unraveled me from him and placed me on a fallen log. I held the slit together and tried to pull up the bodice.

Timothy took off his red jacket and handed it to me. "I think Cara may have something a bit warmer for you when we reach camp." He sat down next to me. "Did he hurt you?" Timothy looked me in the eye.

"No, not really. I don't think today will be easily forgotten tough." I sniffled and tried to draw myself back together.

I must be strong to live in the new world. I need to adjust to this kind of living. I tucked my hair behind my ears.

"You guys are going to have to teach me how to fight. If this is what the world looks like, I'll end up dead before we get to wherever we are going." I said.

He took my hand. "We will, I promise."

I squeezed his hand. "I lost my boots." I wriggled my toes in front of him.

He chuckled. "I see that, I will find you some tomorrow, hopefully. I'm sure I will get tired of lugging you around."

He stood and lifted me. This time he held me in front of him. I rested my head on his chest. My feet were freezing, but the constant swaying somehow managed to lull me to sleep.

I dreamt of the ocean, it was my favorite place in the world. The day was warm and the water sparkled like a million sapphires. The waves were calm, they lapped at the shoreline. My skin felt salty and sun-kissed. I walked to the edge of the water and dipped a toe into the shallows. It was cool and refreshing. I felt like it invited me to walk in further.

The wind began to blow harder. It whipped my hair around my face. A strange rumble shook the ground. It wasn't a Roar, but more like a small earthquake. The sand began to shift beneath me so I plunged further into the water. I turned to the beach and hands emerged from the sand. In shock, I walked backwards to move away from them.

The hands grabbed at the sand. Then arms and then heads of a thousand people rose from the ground. All of them had their pitch-black eyes fixed on me. I ran further out into the waves that now dragged me toward the shore. I fought the waves; I swam against them as hard as I could, but the waves were winning. The people now waited for me to be delivered to them. A line of figures stood down the beach as far as I could see.

I was shaken awake, gasping for air. Timothy had a finger on my lips. "We are here. It's okay." He soothed and laid me on a board above the ground.

My eyes focused on my new surroundings. I saw that we were in a cave. A small fire flickered from the opposite side with the smoke venting through a small hole in the rock above. Cara poked at the fire, her back to me.

"Is she okay?" Cara asked.

Timothy answered for me. "I think she is a little shaken up."

Cara looked at me. "I am glad you are okay. Just don't pull that wandering off crap again."

"I won't, promise." I sat up and yawned. "Trust me, I learned my lesson."

Cara groaned at the sight of the torn sequin dress. "Really, who has something lying around like that?"

"Apparently, a creep that likes playing king of the world." I replied.

She threw her sack to me. "Well, I had hoped to surprise you in a couple of days with these, but I think you need them now," Cara teased.

I opened it to find a long sleeve t-shirt, jeans, and a red hoodie. I almost cried. I checked the sizes and they would fit.

"You sleep pretty hard." She shrugged.

"Thank you." I clung to the clothes.

"I have an extra pair of boots that might be a little on the small side, but they will work till we get to some where we can get you a pair." She offered. When she let her softer side show, it made me smile.

"You have no idea how happy I will be to get out of this ridiculous thing." I smirked.

"I have to ask." Timothy said and sat next to me. He put a finger in the hole at my ribs.

"Mira told me that the last girl Elijah had dinner with displeased him." I said scornfully. "I guess that jerk will need to find a new dress and a new girl."

The thought of Elijah parading girls in his presence bothered me. I'm not even sure why I made the joke.

"Everyone kept saying how he doesn't like his girls all marked-up. I'm glad he didn't get a look at this." I pulled the dress over my knee to expose my scar.

They looked at the mark on my leg. Timothy knelt to have a closer look.

"Mira, that wench, she had something to do with this?" She boiled with anger.

Cara hardly paid attention to anything past Mira. She wasn't concerned with my scar. Cara distracted me from the anger of Elijah and redirected it to Mira.

I brushed Timothy off and shook my head at him. I didn't want the attention on me.

"Yes, but can we wait till tomorrow for me to tell you about it? I really want to change and sort out the day in my own head." I yawned.

They nodded. I could tell Cara held onto her anger though. She huffed and sighed a few times as I put on the new clothes. In the end, she tossed an extra pair of socks at me.

She pursed her lips and snarled. "I have to say it, or I'll explode, if I ever see Elijah again."

"Cara." Timothy interrupted. "Not tonight."

She pouted by the flames. Timothy made his way over to the wooden bed. It was big enough for all of us. I was glad we would sleep together, for the warmth and security. Timothy motioned for me to scoot over and I did.

His closeness made my senses peak. Every time we were close, we seemed to be in survival mode. Now that he was close and I had time to feel his warmth; it was nice. I could smell him; the earthy smell was sweeter than before. I wished he would hold me.

Today had been terrifying. Elijah was a monster. I remembered the irony when Sadie said that my companions were monsters.

I stopped my thoughts from wandering too far into the events of the day. If I reviewed the situation, it allowed the fear back inside of my head. I locked the pain and fear away. I was safe for now.

"Don't stay awake too much longer. We will be leaving at sunrise." He told Cara.

He nuzzled into my back. I felt safe because of them; the thought made me smile. They were rough around the edges, but there was no one else I'd rather be out here with. Timothy had come back for me. He had shown me he cared many times over by the things he not only said, but also the things he did.

Chapter Fifteen

Morning came way too fast. Timothy moved first He yawned and stretched beside me. Cara was snuggled against my front. Her breath was still slow and steady with sleep. I wondered how long she had sulked before she went to sleep.

Timothy walked softly to the embers left from the fire and kicked dirt over it. He left the cave briefly. I noticed his hesitation before he went out into the open. He returned and saw that I had turned and was awake.

He crouched next to me. “I know you said it last night, but I need you to look me in the eyes and tell me again. Tell me that you won’t ever leave without one of us again.” He put his hand around my shoulder.

"I promise." I said earnestly. "I am so sorry for all of the problems I caused." My eyes filled with tears.

He kissed me on the head. "You have no idea how badly I wanted to attack everyone in the room when you made the switch for me. I was so afraid I wouldn't get back to you in time. Cara made me promise to wait until dark, because we both knew the advantages I would have then."

"I know you did what you had to." I blushed. I felt Cara move and waited to see if we woke her. "Cara made a good point. She said you two had a better chance of saving me than we had of rescuing you."

He nodded. "Cara doesn't always show the way she feels about people very well. She does care about you. I also think she cares about you, because she knows I do."

"I know you do; I wouldn't have traded myself for you if I didn't care about you." I said.

It sounded dumb and awkward as soon as I said it, but I meant it. The two of them were my only friends in this world. I loved them both for that.

Cara groaned. "Are you two done with all that mushy junk so I can stop pretending to be asleep?"

We all laughed at ourselves and began to get our act together. Cara handed out a dried biscuit and some dried berries to each of us for breakfast. At least the stop at the village had paid off, some.

"Miss Princess must've had a decent meal last night." She poked at me.

"It was good, once I got over the fear of possibly being poisoned." I relented.

Timothy gave her a look of warning. I put my hand on his arm to show it was okay.

We used a mix Cara bought to brush our teeth with our fingers. It felt amazing to wipe the grime from my teeth.

"I can't believe that with the all of the technology your people had they haven't figured out how to bring back toothbrushes." Cara teased.

"When we get home, that is what we should do." Timothy laughed. "We can stop being fetchers and make toothbrushes for a living."

"Hey, if it will keep you guys around." I stopped. It wasn't fair of me to even wish them to stay with me.

Timothy started pooling our supplies together. I had hoped he kept the sword from last night but I didn't see it anywhere. I had thought it would make a good weapon for me. I had to learn to fight. I wouldn't be caught unable to defend myself again.

The boots Cara gave me squished my toes. I knew I would have blisters by the end of the day, but there would be no complaints. I would earn my keep today after all the trouble I had caused.

The morning sun shone through the trees. We could see our breath in the air but it seemed a little warmer today. Maybe they were wrong and it was closer to spring than they predicted.

Our eyes scanned the landscape to make sure no one from the village had followed us out this far. It was unlikely, but not impossible. We kept quiet just in case.

Cara spotted a squirrel on the ground ahead of us. It dug up acorns that were buried before winter. She put a finger to her lips and held up a hand for us to stop.

Cara walked softly to where she could get a good shot at the squirrel. Her knife flipped in the air and landed in the squirrel. Cara pulled her knife from the animal and draped it over her shoulder. The dead squirrel bounced limply as she walked.

A while later, I decided it was safe enough to talk. "Elijah told me about his arrangement with your people."

Timothy and Cara looked at each other.

"One more reason why we should have never trusted him." Cara said scornfully.

I told them about my time in Elijah's house. I began to describe the isolation cell, my experience of the bath, and then dinner. It turned out that Timothy was held in the same space as I was. He had met the guard with no tongue.

Unfortunately, Elijah didn't have the same concern about marking up his male guests as much as he did his female ones. Timothy endured a beating and a couple broken ribs. Luckily, Cara had some of the healing medicine for him. That was part of the reason she made him wait to come for me. He had needed the time for his bones to mend.

"How much further do we have before we make it home?" I asked.

"If we don't run in to any trouble, it should be maybe three or four days. Most of the time we will be heading east, toward the coast." Timothy cocked his head.

A grin played on my lips.

Timothy smiled back and nodded.

Cara spotted another squirrel ahead. This time she waved me to her. She took out her knife. "Hold it by the handle and throw it like this." She showed me how and handed it to me.

Cara took my bundle so that I could move more quietly. I tried to walk the same way that Cara had earlier while hunting. When the time came, I threw the knife and surprisingly it struck the squirrel. It had not been as clean of a kill, though. Cara ran ahead to finish the job so that the poor thing wouldn't suffer more than needed.

"Not bad for your first time." Timothy put an arm around my shoulders and squeezed.

Around midday, we found a spot that was out of the way to sit and eat. Cara divided our rations and we rested for a bit.

"Timothy, why are you so strong? I mean, if Cara is your sister, shouldn't she be too?" I dared to ask.

"Oh, don't you worry your pretty little head, I'm strong enough if I need to be." Cara narrowed her eyes at me.

I held up my hands in surrender.

Timothy popped her in the arm. "Calm down there, you know what she means." He rubbed his eyes. "Cara and I are siblings, but only half. New generations are bred for purpose. We share the same mother and different fathers. She was bred and trained to be a healer. I was bred and trained for strength."

"So, did you grow up together?" I questioned.

"No, children are taken from their mothers on their third birthday to be trained. From then on, we live among our specialty groups." Cara spoke softly. I saw pain in her eyes. "I only know Timothy is my brother because he got hurt and was my patient. A blood sample came back from the scientists with his genetic background showing our link to the same woman."

"Wow." I shook my head. "I can't even imagine."

"It is what it is." Cara shrugged. She loaded herself up and headed off.

Timothy watched her with sympathy. "She is still very angry at our people. They told us lies so that we would work toward enslaving and destroying humanity. I am sure many people would have simply chosen to leave if they had known that some things are worth saving up here." He took my hand and helped me stand.

"Honestly, since we left the compound, I haven't met many humans worth saving." I said, dejected.

"I met one." He winked at me. I blushed.

Chapter Sixteen

We walked behind Cara. She needed some space, but not too much that we couldn't keep an eye on her. She kept her head low and appeared to be looking for more small game.

Timothy showed me types of plants that could be eaten. He continued to point out others that could be used for medicinal purposes. Some were better used for building or weaving. I tried to make note of a few of the ones that sounded important in case I needed them one day.

Timothy bent down to show me a plant called squirrel tail that can be used for excessive bleeding. I squatted next to him and carefully pulled the plant out of the ground, roots and all. I handed it to Timothy and he stuffed it into my pack.

We looked ahead to follow Cara. She wasn't there. Maybe she was hidden behind a tree and waited to scare us. I recalled the night

I first met her when she jumped out of a tree and almost scared us to death. Cara had thought she was funny, but it gave me a jolt I hadn't forgotten.

I saw the fear in Timothy's eyes and I took his hand. I signaled him to stay quiet. He read the mischievous look on my face and we crept to the next thick tree. We split and peeked around it. No Cara.

"Get your hands up and don't make any quick movements." A voice startled us.

I looked out of the corner of my eye and saw Timothy raise his hands and take a step away from the trunk. I copied his movements. I leaned my head back. I was getting tired of these stupid human games. Everyone wanted something, human or mole. I rolled my eyes.

"Darn it, I think we got two of them on Elijah's list." A hardened female voice said.

"Where's the other one?" The man asked.

Timothy shrugged. "I don't know, she disappeared."

"I don't like that Billy. I don't like it at all. She might have dug herself under the ground or something." The woman's voice waivered.

"You better call for her boy! I am not out here messing around." Billy walked up behind Timothy and put a gun to his head.

He poked the gun into Timothy's skull. He wore a faded flannel shirt and baggy jeans held up by a cinched belt. He was sickeningly skinny, his eyes, and cheek bones sunken.

"Cara! Cara! Better, come out here. This guy has a gun pointed at my head!" He yelled.

Billy kicked Timothy in the heel. Timothy fell to the ground. I tried to remain calm.

"Dang it, son!" He shouted. "You shouldn't have said anything about the gun." He stood over Timothy. "You call her." He waved the gun at me.

"Cara, please!" I pled.

We all waited for noise or for her to come out. She didn't and I hoped she had a plan.

Billy yanked Timothy up by his hood. "Obviously, one of your little girlfriends doesn't care too much for you. Jean, get that girl over here. You need to cover her."

The woman approached me and wrapped an arm around my neck. She smelled rotten and her frame was like Billy's.

"You better not try a thing." She snapped and held a knife out for me to see. It looked strange in her bony hand.

"Let's get these two tied up and see if we can persuade our girl to come out." Billy decided.

Jean tied a rope around my hands and tethered it to Timothy's wrists. Timothy looked worried, which didn't help me trying to keep my composure. They sat us on the ground beside one another. Jean was in front and Billy at our backs.

"Girl, you come out now, you hear? I don't want to get desperate, but I am not leaving you out there! Elijah wants all of you. He ain't going to settle for some." Billy sounded nervous.

Billy reached over us and held out his hand to Jean. She gave him the blade.

"Alright now, I tried to be civil about this. Now you're going to make me do bad things to your people." Billy yelled. He held the knife between us. "Are we going to start with the boy or girl?" He said loudly.

Timothy squirmed a bit at that.

"Aw, look at that." Billy teased. "The mole don't like the thought of his girl getting marked up neither."

"I say you start with the boy, that way we hopefully don't have to do much to her." Jean said.

"As you wish my dear." Billy agreed. He slid the blade along Timothy's forearm.

Timothy groaned when the cut was made. I couldn't help myself and screamed at the sight of his blood. It spread across his arm and dripped onto the ground.

"If you kill him, Elijah will be pissed." I blurted out. "You know what he does to people that make him mad?"

"Shut up!" Jean slapped me across the face. My lip quivered.

Timothy hunched over and swayed a bit. The muscles in his jaw clenched in pain.

"Is that enough you disgusting mole?" Billy hollered.

Still there was no answer from Cara. I searched the woods in front of me for a sign that she was there. I saw nothing but a few leaves trickle from different trees.

"I told you I don't like this, Billy. I feel like she is watching us. It gives me the creeps." Jean shivered.

"You got no stomach for this stuff, woman. I knew I shouldn't bring you along." He scolded.

"You can't cut that boy as bad next time or he isn't going to make it back." She motioned at Timothy.

Billy moved behind me now. "I'm going to ask you again; get out here or I'm cutting the girl!"

Jean gave him a warning glance. I started to breathe shallower and began to shake.

Timothy looked up at Billy. "I would suggest you don't do that."

Billy huffed and quickly swiped the blade across my back. I cried out and fell forward. Timothy growled deeply, from the bottom of his chest. His hands slipped from the rope. He sprang upon Billy; blood sprayed all over. I couldn't tell the difference between the warm blood that spread across my back and his blood on me.

Billy and Timothy landed on the ground with a loud crack. Jean fell in front on me. Her face landed next to mine. Her eyes were wide in surprise and blank with death. I wailed and rolled onto my back to get away from her face.

Timothy straddled Billy, but I could only see Timothy's back and Billy's legs under him. Cara leapt over me and onto Billy. My sight faded into tunnel vision. My head hit the ground and I lay sprawled in an awkward position. I stared above me and with every blink, the light dimmed.

Timothy fell beside me. He shook me and hugged me. I moaned from pain. I remembered being turned over, my leg burned, and then darkness came over me.

Chapter Seventeen

Timothy was next to me. His body faced mine. I reached for him but my hand hit a barrier. I flattened my palm against it. It was hardened plastic between us.

Panic ran through my gut, I had to get to him. I hit the partition and yelled for him; he didn't wake up. I turned my head and noticed that I was encased in a box. I realized that there were wires and tubes hooked into my chest and head.

My eyes darted to my other surroundings. We were in a room that was stark white with machines lining one wall. An alarm went off and I heard, "Alex, Alex," through an intercom.

I sat up straight, eyes wide and heaving for breath.

"Alex, Alex!" Timothy called to me. He cradled me. "It's okay. You are okay."

I took in my surroundings. We were in a room with wooden walls. I relaxed a bit and allowed Timothy to hold me. My heart and breath slowed.

I pulled one of his arms in front of me. I could feel dried blood on his skin. "Are you alright?" I asked.

He smiled. "Of course, thanks to Cara."

Cara came to stand over me. "Yeah, I do what I can."

"What took you so long?" I joked.

"I had to have the right moment or those hillbillies would have killed all of us." She rubbed her hands together. "They were idiot bounty hunters."

I closed my eyes and Timothy kissed me lightly on the head. When I reopened them, Cara was gone and Timothy filled my sight.

"How many times do you think we will apologize for getting each other hurt?" He squinted at me.

"Hopefully, not many more, because I don't know how much more of this I can take." I confessed.

He laid his head on my stomach and sighed. I put my hand in his hair and listened to Cara move about the room.

I took a moment to savor the calm. "Where are we?"

Timothy answered without moving. "A tree house we built some time ago. It is out of our way but it was the safest place I could think of."

"Mmhmm." I acknowledged.

Cara spoke next. "We built this place when we were moving people south, in the beginning of our fetching days." She walked over to me and put a hand on my head. "I had to put you out for two days." She gave me an apologetic grin. "I patched you up but had to take care of Timothy first. We wouldn't have made it anywhere if he wasn't able to carry you."

"How far did you carry me?" I tapped Timothy on the head.

"About one of the two days." He said. "You were healing that day."

"Those morons had no idea what they were doing. If I hadn't had my salves you both would have bled out." Cara remarked.

"Thank you for not letting us die." I said.

"Meh, don't mention it." She shrugged me off. "I don't think Timothy would forgive me if I had let you go."

He swatted at her.

"So, what's the plan, now?" I questioned.

"We will wait a day or two for you both to regain your strength. As soon as you are able,

I am going to take a few hours to show you how to handle a knife. I took Jean's, I don't think she will need it anymore." Cara said callously.

My back was still sore but I could tell I was on the mend. I brushed Timothy off my stomach and rolled over. He crawled up beside me and laid his arm across me. In seconds, I was asleep again.

I must've slept through that night, too. Whatever Cara had given me to knock me out almost worked too well.

My eyes opened in a haze. I shuffled around and realized I was alone. Being alone made me nervous.

Cara and Timothy became a part of me that I feared to be without.

I crawled back into our makeshift bed. My back didn't hurt anymore. I wondered if there was even a scar.

Last night, I had been too tired and groggy to look over Timothy arms in any detail. All I knew was that we were okay and that was enough.

Finally, I heard noises below on the ground. I softly sank onto the floor and pressed my face on the boards. I could see Timothy as he scaled the trunk. There were notches in the wood he used to hoist himself. I sat back in relief.

Timothy lowered his head to come through the entryway. He smiled when he spotted me awake. He placed a satchel of food on my lap. I didn't hesitate and eagerly unfolded it to find a cooked fish and dried squirrel meat.

"Sorry." He apologized. "There isn't much else right now. It looks like we will be waiting a bit for fruit. It's still a little too cold here for it to grow naturally."

I didn't care what I ate. I needed to put something in my stomach. It did raise the question of how the village grew food in the cold though. I asked Timothy and he told me it was an advancement that his people had shared with Elijah, as part of his negotiations.

"You have to give it to the guy, he is smart." I said with my mouth full.

"Humph." Timothy grumbled. He sat on the floor next to me.

"Your people are also smart." I stated.

Timothy avoided the odd compliment. "The other meat is from one of the squirrels. Cara, the resourceful, had pinned one to a tree during the attack to save for us."

"She amazes me." I swallowed. "Both of you do."

He plucked a small morsel of the fish in my hand and ate it. "Of all the food, fish is my least favorite up here." He sighed.

"I am not the biggest fan either, but I have no clue how long it's been since I ate last. I could eat fourteen fish in one sitting. I am that hungry." I exaggerated.

He poked me in the ribs. "Fourteen, huh?"

I giggled and he handed me a bladder of water. I drank way too fast and gagged.

"Slow down." Timothy ordered. "You'll make yourself sick." He took the water from me. "You haven't eaten in days so take it easy."

I groaned at his overprotective behavior. I chuckled, nonetheless, because he was right. I did pace myself from that point on. The fish went down well so I didn't want to chance it coming back up.

Timothy lifted himself onto the bed. "Let's have a look at your back."

I slid the loose shirt up my spine and to the base of my neck. "How big was the cut?"

He lightly touched one shoulder blade and traced his finger down to the bottom of my rib cage. There he placed his palm open against my side. His touch and the knowledge of how large of a wound gave me goosebumps.

He pulled me back into him and wrapped his arms around my shoulders. I could smell the blood again. There had been so much of our blood everywhere. The memory, made my stomach turn.

"They were idiots. There was no need for them to hurt you. I thought I was calling a bluff; I swear I really didn't think he would do it." Timothy whispered into my ear, full of regret.

"It wasn't your fault. Obviously, they were desperate." I reassured him. I leaned into his embrace.

"That's not a gamble I will take again. I promised I wouldn't allow anyone to hurt you. I take that seriously, but I let you down." He spoke through a lump in his throat.

"Timothy, you already apologized." I replied. "It is done. I will learn to fight so this won't happen to me or you again."

I pushed back the sleeve on his arm to see the damage that was done to him. A jagged, white line ran across his muscles. I mimicked the way he traced my wound. I kissed the scar gently. He sucked in air and rested his head on me. I moved to the other arm and kissed the mark across it too.

Timothy bent down and scooped me up onto his lap. He looked at me in a way I had never had someone look at me before. I swear he could see my heart beat through my eyes.

He brushed a few strands of hair from my face and kissed my lips. My heart pounded in my ears and blood rushed to my face. He laid me on the bed, looked over me with an unreadable expression, and then left hastily.

What in the heck was that? What had I done? I hadn't planned on kissing him, ever. I didn't even know if we were the same species, for God's sake. Not to mention the fact that he had been paid to rescue me. A rush of embarrassment over took me. I had gone and complicated things.

I bit my bottom lip. I could still feel the kiss. It had been sweet and exhilarating, but at what cost? If there was one rule that always rang true, it was that for every action there is an equal and opposite reaction. Now he was gone and whatever drove him to leave was partially my fault. I slapped the bed beside me in frustration.

Cara walked in just in time to see me slap the bed. "What is going on? I passed Timothy on my way to the tree and he greeted me with a grunt and I come in here to see you fighting with the bed." She frowned.

"Oh God, Cara, I kissed him. I mean he kissed me. Ugh!" I swore.

She held up a hand. "Wait, for it." She hunched over dramatically. "Ew. On top of that, ok, makes total sense." She shrugged.

"Well, your brother gave me a strange look and then left, so that was a little weird." I said sarcastically.

She plopped on the bed. "Did you just eat the fish, because that might be it." She joked.

"Forget it Cara." I snarled and turned my back to her.

"Okay, okay." She rubbed my arm. "It is just since we left below ground Timothy has always made his life about business. He wanted to make a difference for your people and he thinks he can't have anything that he cares about because it might keep him from doing that. Alex, you are blind if you can't see that he has been caring for you more and more."

"I have too." I admitted. "I care about both of you."

Cara opened her mouth to make an inappropriate joke.

I cut her off. "You know what I mean. I guess I do have feelings for Timothy and that scares me."

She patted my shoulder. "It'll work itself out. Give him a little time and you two can figure it out. Maybe it's a good thing, maybe not. We will still have each other's backs."

"Thanks, Cara." I smiled at her.

She went over to the other side of the room and took her knife from the bag. She brought a stone from her pocket and began to sharpen it. The sound grated on me at first and then the rhythm of her strokes became melodic. Cara quietly hummed to the beat.

I laughed at myself. “What?” Cara looked insulted.

“No, not you; it dawned on me that here I am worrying about a boy when less than a week ago I was worried about the Roar taking me. That is how long it took me to become so dense.” I said in a self-loathing voice.

“Goes to show you, we are all creatures that focus on the present.” She grinned. She returned to sharpening and humming.

Chapter Eighteen

Timothy returned later in the day. I was hopeful when I saw the proud look on his face.

"I got us a boar." He boasted.

"Where is it?" Cara eagerly asked.

"I went for a run and came across one. It's downstairs. Can you help me with it Cara? I thought we would take it to the pond and clean it." He avoided my eyes.

"Sure, but I think some fresh air would do Alex some good. Are you alright to bring her down?" Cara winked at me.

"Um, I guess, Alex, you up for it?" He asked.

"I would love to get out for a bit." I answered.

I shuffled out of the door and to the trunk behind them. Timothy crouched so I could get on to his back. I still was light-headed from loss of blood and lack of food. He descended carefully and paused often to make sure I had a good grip.

At the bottom, he set me on the ground and held my arm to steady me. We all walked through some brush to a small pond not far away. I noticed that I ran out of breath easier than before. I was glad neither of them brought it up.

The boar was laid on the ground. It had to be a juvenile male. He was a good size, but had small tusks and looked young.

Cara guided me to a stump on the edge of the pond. They had used the rest of the tree to build the treehouse. I sat and watched them get to work.

"It looks like we will have bacon tonight kids!" Cara exclaimed. She clapped her hands together.

My mouth watered at the thought of fried bacon. I could use the fat and calories. I tried to relax, but kept a good ear out to the forest.

"How far did you go?" Cara asked Timothy.

"A few miles south," he said while he skinned the carcass.

"You see any signs of people?" Cara continued.

"I saw gray smoke further south. It looked like it wasn't anything for us to worry about though." He looked up at me. "At this time of the day, no one is traveling far."

They had the skin off and began to gut the hog.

"I already drained it."

I wasn't sure how he did that so fast. I nodded at him.

"Elijah told me the machines are broken, is that true?" I asked bravely.

They stopped and stretched.

"Yes, for now." Cara agreed.

"What else did Elijah tell you?" Timothy prodded. He wiped his hands on a rag.

"That's it, he only told me about his bargain with your people, and that the big machines were broken for now." I shrugged. "Oh, I almost forgot, he did say something about the energy source needing replenished. You told me that my camp was an energy camp. Do the two correlate?"

Timothy looked weary. "That doesn't make sense. We had tons of ore and fossil fuel stored."

"Unless the engineers have decided alterations may make the machines work more efficiently." Cara explained. "They were always looking for ways to replace the mines."

They both cleaned and stripped the meat. I could tell they were both deep in thought. Both of their wrinkled brows announced it. It was one of the few times you could tell they were siblings.

"So, something has been bothering me." I pried, gently. "I get that they use us for slave labor, but I never found out where the people go that disappear?"

"Oh my God, Timothy, that is it!" Cara exclaimed. "I knew that they were working on a way to replace the mines. They were dangerous because of eminent collapsing tunnels. The weight on the surface from humans caused many deaths." She looked at me. "Your people saw the increase in sinkholes over the last decade due to our aggressive digging."

"Cara, are you saying what I think you are?" Timothy plopped down. His eyes pled for the connection he made to be wrong.

She froze as she pieced the puzzle together in her mind.

"What? What?" I stammered.

"Good lord, they are using humans to make fuel." Her bottom lip quivered.

Timothy put his head in his hands. I tried to take it in, these creatures had not only harvested our lives, but they were also harvesting us. I stared at my lap and watched drops of tears as they collected into a spot on my pants. No one moved or spoke as we worked through the details silently.

"Your people could do that?" I cried. "They could use us for the energy inside us?"

"The technology was being formed before we left. I didn't understand it then. Most down there believe humans to be expendable." Cara's voice was small.

I had never seen her this way. She was weak and helpless.

Timothy sat there and his face. He was clearly distraught as well.

"How do they do it?"

"The engineers and scientists were planning on a way to use bodies to make fuels. Under great pressure and heat, which is in abundance down there, it is possible to make large amounts, quickly.

There was another idea they tossed around. The brain and nervous system works off electrical pulses. That would take more time and space-."

"Stop." Timothy cut her off.

I couldn't stand to sit there with them anymore. I was repulsed by the actions of their people. Their people had gone beyond comprehension to commit genocide. It was clear that they would extinguish all of us and use our flesh and bone for their benefit. I knew it wasn't Cara or Timothy's fault, but I needed to be alone. On wobbly legs, I got up and shuffled in the direction of the treehouse.

Cara reached out for me.

"Please, give me a minute." I requested.

She stepped back, her mouth opened and closed while she tried to find words. I parted the bushes and moved through.

"I'm so sorry." Cara said to my back.

I ignored her and shuffled back to the tree. I was out of breath long before I reached it. The treehouse could've been in the clouds because there was no way I was going to be able to climb the notches.

I sank to the ground and cried for my people; the individuals I had already lost, those that had become animals in this new world, and those still being taken by our enemies. This wasn't even a war; there was no fighting them. This was a slaughter.

My body curled into the fetal position. My day would come, too. The moles would have every one of us. They would use everything we had so that they would own the Earth.

Eventually, I wore myself out. No more tears would come. I shut my eyes and slept. It was the first time, nightmares didn't find me.

"Come on." Cara shook me. "It's time for your first lesson." She laid Jean's knife beside me.

"Are you serious?" I lifted my head.

"I'm very serious. You can use your anger to try and kill me." Cara cocked her head sideways.

"I don't want to kill you. What use would that be? As far as I know, there are millions of moles lining up for the chance to kill all of us. What am I going to do against that?" I asked.

"For one, you can at least put up a good fight." She raised an eyebrow. "Get up and fight me."

I took the hilt of the knife she held out in my hand. Cara offered a hand to me and hoisted me up.

"It's time to get to work." She grinned.

The knife dragged into the dirt as I stood. I saw it carve a distinct line, like the ones on Timothy's arms. The irony of me being its new owner crossed my thoughts.

"We will only work on stance and slicing." She positioned my hands on the base. "I want you to be my reflection. Do exactly as I do, ok?"

I nodded. She stepped back in front of me. Cara spread her legs a little and planted her feet. I copied her movements. She raised her arms and thrust them down. I did the same.

"Good, put a little more strength behind it." She advised.

I slashed the blade down again this time with all my might. The knife made a whistling noise.

Cara pointed at the knife. "That is the sound you want to hear every time you bring it down."

I grit my teeth and repeated the motion several times. The length of the blade felt balanced in my hand. It felt like an extension of me.

Cara looked pleased. "Why don't we move over to the bushes and see how she cuts?" My back stung as a reminder that I knew how this thing could cut.

I raised the knife and released my hatred on the bush. The blade sliced through the twigs easily. I did it over and over until I couldn't lift the knife anymore.

"Now that is how you trim foliage, folks." Cara teased.

We laughed together.

"I am not sure how to make this better." Cara confessed. "I can only tell you that I will fight against my own people to keep you alive. What they are doing isn't right. It goes against everything they indoctrinated in us. Preserve the world and its inhabitants."

She took my hand. "We are the same misguided society that you have known. Take what you believe belongs to you. Kill for it if need be. I don't agree with that brainwashing."

"Listen, I get that we humans make mistakes. I admitted the other night that I haven't met a decent human since the end of the world. We screwed up our planet and your people felt the need to put us in our place. At least, that's how I see it, but I have too many good memories of my people to think our extinction is necessary."

"Tell me some." She begged. "Please, I don't have many pleasant memories from where I come from or here either." She sat down and pulled me with her.

I studied her face to make sure she meant it. Her eyes became glossy and pooled around the edges. I kept her hand in mine.

"I remember my mom tucking me into bed at night. She would kiss me on the head and I knew she loved me." I started.

Cara squeezed my fingers.

"Holidays were the best. My family would all get together, aunts, uncles, cousins, and grandparents. It was so nice to see everyone all at once. We played games and caught each other up about what had been going on in our lives. My favorite part was listening to stories about things that had happened a long time ago, when the older people reminisced."

"We don't have older people down there." Cara explained. "We were always told that they were sent to a far section to be taken care of, but I knew better."

"I am sorry that you didn't get to know them. The old people can be wise; they have seen a lot." I told her.

"My people always focused on the future. That is why we didn't stay with our mothers very long." She revealed.

"That's funny, because when I think about it, most of us tried to learn from the past and worried about the present. Not many lived for the future." I realized that this may be the main difference between our thought processes.

Timothy emerged from the tree line. I hadn't noticed the sun lowered in the sky. He carried a slab of meat at his side.

"Is everything alright?" He asked when he spotted us together.

"Yes, we were contemplating life and our existence. That's all." Cara told him.

"I don't know if I can handle anymore life epiphanies today." He sighed and helped both of us to our feet.

"Me either." I agreed. "When do we eat?"

"As soon as I can get this cooked." He gestured to the meat.

"Let's get a fire going." She cracked her fingers.

They started a fire in no time. Timothy rolled over a few stumps left from building the treehouse. It was cozy near the warmth of the fire. The smell of our dinner tugged at my stomach. I was still ravenous from my days without food.

Once dinner was prepared, we huddled together to eat. The boar had been a luxury bestowed to us. Every bite was savored by moans and grunts. I ate until I was uncomfortable and had to prop myself back for my stomach to not hurt.

The firelight danced between us and reminded me that we are all in this together. There was no them or me, it was "us".

Cara excused herself to bed shortly after the meal ended. There was an awkward air between Timothy and me. It had to end, I hated it being there. We had gone too far together for a kiss to ruin our comradery.

"I shouldn't have kissed your arms; if it made you upset I am sorry." I offered.

He squirmed. "Trust me this has nothing to do with how it felt, Alex. I shouldn't have kissed you for a million reasons, you kissing my arms, wasn't the problem."

That surprised me. "Then what was it?"

"All of this is difficult. I wasn't supposed to feel this way about you. I have always been so good at separating what I do, from feeling. You have blurred that line." He confessed and closed his eyes.

"I'm not entirely sure how I feel about it either." I admitted. "It seems every day I learn something that should make me more nervous about you. For heaven's sake, your people are committing genocide against mine."

He pinched the bridge of his nose. "I know. It's ridiculous, yet it happened."

"We have to do what we have to do. Let's make a pact." I announced. I held out my hand. "We won't kiss again."

He laughed at me, but shook my hand anyway. I stuffed my hands in my pockets. "So now that's done, would you mind taking me to bed?"

Timothy grinned. "Of course."

He tossed me onto his back and scaled the tree trunk with ease. Cara already breathed softly, asleep. He laid me down next to her.

I mouthed. "Thank you."

He winked at me and went back below.

"Is everything better?" Cara scared me. I thought she was asleep.

"Yeah, but we decided no more kissing. We have too much to worry about. Romance isn't on the top of the list." I crinkled my nose.

"Sounds good to me." She yawned and curled into a ball.

Chapter Nineteen

The smell of bacon tickled my nose. My mouth watered before my eyes even opened. I moaned and stretched. My head didn't seem as foggy as it had since the injury.

"Come on lazy bones! Breakfast is ready!" Timothy called from below.

I scratched and shuffled to the trunk. My hair stood out in all directions. I tried to smooth it down.

Cara and Timothy looked up at me.

"I've had enough! Alex, you are getting a bath today!" Cara teased.

"Is it that bad?" I asked.

Timothy nodded at me with a look of apology.

"Do you need help down?" He asked and walked to the tree.

"Nope, I'm going to try it today." I said proudly.

"Just take it easy, I'll be right here." Timothy cautioned.

I carefully plotted my route before I left the platform. I stepped onto the first set of notches and eased my foot down until I could feel the next. My arms and legs shook from lack of strenuous use. It must have bothered Timothy, too, because he positioned himself directly below me.

At the second to the last wrung, I pushed myself off the tree. I dropped about five feet and Timothy caught me. He gave me a stern look. I slapped at him and smiled.

"Geez, how dramatic of you two." Cara muttered. I blushed. "Eat then we are going to train. I think you should be fine for traveling tomorrow."

"I'm ready to get moving again. I think if I stay here much longer, I might never want to leave." It seemed like the safest place I had been in a very long time.

The bacon was amazing. I ate more than my share. Timothy waited for me, but grew tired of sitting around. He excused himself to pool supplies. I wondered when my insatiable hunger would cease. I couldn't keep up with it on the move.

"Ok, so today, we are going to work on different ways to defend yourself." Cara told me. "For now, if you can buy one of us some time to get to you in an emergency, you will be fine." I agreed.

She lined up with me again. "No weapons first, I want you to come at me."

"Like how?" I blushed; it seemed silly.

"Like, you are going to try to hit me." She began to get irritated with me.

I charged and swung my fist at her face. She caught it and twisted. The pain brought me to my knees.

"Your turn." Cara said and let me go.

I rubbed my elbow.

She sprang forward, her fist propelled at me. I snagged her, but her fist still clipped my jaw. It was enough to catch me off guard. I let go, before I directed her to the ground.

"Again." Cara demanded.

We went over the movements several times, until I mastered subduing her. Then we went on to the next defensive tactic. I was winded so we stopped frequently for water. I was a fast learner and Cara was pleased with my progress.

"That's enough of that." Cara put her hands on her hips. "I think we both earned a bath."

"Where?" I asked.

"To the pond; I bet I'll beat you there!" She yelled over her shoulder and took off.

I giggled and ran as fast as I could to catch up. My body was strong even if my lungs hadn't caught up from inactivity. I ran through the thicket as Cara kicked her boots off. She pulled off her top with no modesty.

"Are we going in naked?" I asked.

"I honestly don't care. We can leave on our undergarments if it makes you feel better." She chided.

Her pants were thrown over a log. She ran straight in to the water and dove in once the water was deep enough.

I shed my clothes as fast as possible. I wanted to hurry and get in the water. It was still chilly out. No doubt, the water would be cold.

I hung my pants next to Cara's. She already made her way out to the middle of the pond. I sprinted in so I couldn't change my mind once I found out how cold it was. The water was dark and ominous. I swam out to where Cara was laid on her back.

Timothy came into the clearing. He folded his arms across his chest and watched us float about.

"That has got to be freezing." He laughed.

"Yes, it is." I said.

"Get in here! Stop pretending like you don't want to." Cara joked and splashed in his direction.

He pursed his lips. "What if I'm chicken?"

"Stop being a wuss." I stuck my tongue out at him.

"Meh, I won't make you beg me." He peeled off the layers of jacket and shirts.

I couldn't help but notice that he was well built. He was strong and his body reflected that. His muscles pushed and pulled under his skin as he undressed.

Cara splashed at me. "Yoo-hoo, Earth to Alex?" She called.

My face flushed. I dove under the surface and swam under Cara. I pinched her leg and I could hear her muffled yelp. She submerged and wrestled me under the water.

Timothy jumped in from a nearby rock. The waves rocked Cara and I. Timothy joined us. We splashed, played, and acted like normal people for a while.

Timothy put his hands on my waist. My skin prickled from his touch. He tossed me into the air; it was exhilarating. I hit the water and swam back to him. We shoved each other playfully.

Cara made her way out of the pond. She wrung out her hair. "I'm going to get a fire going!" She called.

Timothy raced me to the rock. We climbed up and took turns making silly poses as we jumped. It was so good to laugh and enjoy things. I smiled at Timothy and spit the water from my mouth.

I wrapped my arms around his shoulders. He held me as he tread-water. I placed my head on his shoulder. My hair fanned out around me with the waves.

"We should get out before hypothermia sets in." He whispered in my ear.

"Besides we might end up doing something dumb, like kiss again." I swallowed.

He poked me in the ribs. "We wouldn't want that, would we? Let's go."

He took my hands, put them on his shoulders, and swam to the shore. His skin was warm even in the frigid water.

Luckily, Cara came back just then with a blanket to wrap around us. It was another good excuse to get close to him. He rubbed my arms and back to dry them, at the same time it gave me heat. When he made his way to my legs, he paused at the line along my shin. He ran a finger along it and looked up at me.

"I know it looks bad, but I don't even remember how I got it." I shrugged. "It bothers me though."

His brow furrowed as he studied it. "I saw it before, but you disregarded it. Cara should look at that. Maybe she has something that could help it."

We made our way to the fire in tandem. Cara had taken our clothes to wash them. Our undergarments would have to dry with us by the fire. It was time that I got over my issues with indecency. When it came down to it, in the scheme of things it was nothing.

The flames danced to the tune that Cara hummed. I recognized the tune as the same from last time she hummed. It seemed to be a lullaby of sorts, meant to soothe the listener. I picked at the meat and sparse greens Cara had prepared. The song and warmth made me drowsy.

The sun had set and the sky burned with the colors of the fire. It reminded me that the moles hadn't taken everything from me. I smiled to myself in defiance.

"So, are we ready tomorrow then?" Cara asked abruptly.

"Yeah, we should start early. I was thinking maybe we could try to get to the river by tomorrow night?" Timothy said.

She nodded. "Hopefully."

Timothy handed me my knife.

"One more time, against me?" He prompted.

I looked to Cara. She waved at me to go. The long knife was heavier in my hand because I was so tired. Cara handed Timothy her knife.

"You two, be careful, though. I don't need to get stuck patching one of you up again so soon." She huffed.

There we stood in our underwear trying to look serious about sparring. Instead, we were ridiculously bare.

"Let's go, sweet cheeks." He winked at me.

With a groan, I attacked with a lunge forward. He deflected the knife and immediately disarmed me.

"What have you two been doing? Exchanging cookie recipes?" He mocked.

My face went hot with embarrassment.

"Again." He demanded.

I picked up the knife and in the same movement wheeled at him. He parried the blow away from him, but did not make me lose it. His face filled with amusement.

Timothy bent down and swept my feet from under me. I landed on my back with a thud. He stood over me, knife aimed at my chest. I kicked just above his knee and brought him down.

Swiftly, I rose to fighting stance. He scrambled back upright. He dropped the knife and charged. I tossed my weapon, just before he jumped upon me.

Cara taught me to use my hips, so that he couldn't pin me with his knees. I pressed my feet into the ground and rolled him off. Instantly, I rolled in the opposite direction until I was out of reach.

"Good job." He acknowledged me. "You've come a long way."

Cara beamed at us. "Alex is a good student. She learns fast."

I brushed myself off and bowed. They both clapped for me.

"If we run into trouble, do you think I can buy you time?" I asked.

"I would rather not put it to a test, but I do believe so." Timothy grinned. He was proud of my progress.

"Okay, kids, I'm going to take my clothes and head upstairs," I announced. I took my clothes from the stump and made my way up the tree.

"Night," they called after me.

Chapter Twenty

A noise startled me out of the nightmare where I am at the beach with a line of moles that waited for me. I lay in sweat and panted. No one was in the bed with me. I sat up and quietly padded to the entrance of the room, careful to not step on loose boards.

I heard voices below. They belonged to Cara and Timothy, I relaxed a little. Curiosity got the best of me, so I stayed to listen for a minute.

"You really like her, don't you?" Cara whispered.

From the noise of leaves that crunched, I could tell Timothy paced.

"I do. I know it is stupid and careless."

This was good, so I listened further.

"She is pretty and smart. It makes sense, however, I'm not sure how it is going to fit in with our plans." Cara reasoned.

Timothy confessed. “I don’t know. Like I said, it is stupid and completely illogical.”

“Welcome to life, brother. Nothing has ever made sense. We keep running from the logical. I mean, do you really think we are going to make a difference against them?” She paused.

“I don’t know. We would’ve died fighting them below. At least now we have a chance.” Timothy was frustrated.

“I never put it together, that they were going to use people for energy. I swear.” She promised.

There was silence and then the leaves rustled again. I leaned against the door frame.

“I hope we are doing the right thing by taking her back to him.” Timothy worried. “I’ll kill him if he tries to hurt her.”

My stomach knotted. Timothy did know who had commissioned the rescue. Why didn’t he tell me?

“He said she would help.” Cara reassured him.

“I have no reason to believe him. How many times have we been lied to?” He paused. “How many times have we lied?”

“So what, we don’t go back? Make up another story and ride off in to the sunset, taking Alex with us?” Cara questioned.

“We go back, but keep on our toes. It doesn’t feel right, but I don’t see any way around it.”

“I can’t bear the thought of her seeing him. She will be so disappointed.” Cara said softly.

I already felt that way. I wanted to scream at the top of my lungs. How could they lie to me after everything?

They gathered their things. Timothy kicked dirt over the fire. I crept back to the bed. My mouth was dry, my mind filled with a thousand thoughts and questions.

I pretended to be asleep. Cara crawled over me and Timothy lay behind me. I waited until they were both asleep before opening my eyes.

Who had sent them? Why were they worried about my safety with him? I calmed myself by remembering that Timothy had sworn to keep me safe from whoever sent for me, if he tried to hurt me. What plans had I interrupted?

I couldn’t stand the feeling of betrayal; every moment that I had felt uncertain about Timothy and Cara rushed back.

The truth, in finality, was that I was blindly being led into the unknown, by two strangers.

Timothy had said that he would protect me, but to what point, especially, if I was getting in the way. I was embarrassed and hurt that I played into their game.

I resolved to leave. There was no way I was being carted back to someone that might have a plan to hurt me. I certainly wasn't going to stick around and fall for Timothy any more than I had. I was a pawn they had grown attached.

I slid over Timothy. He snorted, but didn't wake. I tiptoed over to a bulging sack by the entrance and lifted it on my back. The knife was by the door so I listened to their breaths as I tucked it between the straps of the bag. Their breaths remained even. My boots were the last to be secured.

Carefully, I climbed down the tree. At the bottom, I oriented myself. The sun set straight ahead so the south must be left. I searched the sky for a star I could use as my compass. One star shone blue and twinkled brightly. I turned and walked that way.

Further South, it would be warmer which was better for me in the long run. I could head south and then to the east. I hoped that I would find the coast that way. I didn't want to end up at the same place as I was being taken, but if I went south a bit, I'd be ok.

My leg started to act up after half an hour. I couldn't understand why it would ache so quickly. The landscape was the same as it had been. The ground leveled from the hills and slopes we had started the trek across many days ago.

I sat against a tree and pulled up my pant leg. A drop of blood oozed from the bottom of the scar. This scared me; it had never done that before. I tore a piece from the bottom of my shirt and tied it around the wound. I needed to make ground before the others woke and noticed my absence.

I continued, slower than at first. My leg still bothered me, but I trudged forward. After every several steps, I reminded myself to listen. That was the key to survival, be aware.

The woods became thicker and it was more difficult to see my guiding star. Blood dripped down my leg and made a small puddle in my boot. I retied the makeshift bandage. I didn't want to spend too much time on the wound. It wouldn't help to confirm the damage.

When I thought I couldn't walk anymore, I pushed harder. The pain was my companion, as selfish as it was. After I passed a few trees, I promised only a few more until I would take a break.

Finally, I gave in to the pain. A hollowed bush would have to be my shelter for the remainder of the night. I squeezed into the low twigs and curled in around my pack. I must've put a few miles between here and the treehouse, at least.

I tried to sleep but every noise startled me. A squirrel ran along the limbs above. An owl hooted from its perch. Dried leaves shuffled and then two raccoons squealed.

At dawn, my surroundings became clearer. Many of the trees were pine, straight and tall. Bushes lined any light that made it to the forest floor which was thick with needles.

It seemed that my leg had stopped bleeding during the night. I dug around in the pack swiped from the treehouse. I needed to take an inventory of supplies. I laid the items around me so that I could keep a visual record. There was a filled water bladder, some dried meat, a shirt, a length of rope, and a small tarp. There were a few essentials but none of Cara's healing concoctions. At least, I had my knife. I stuffed the things back in and chewed a small piece of meat for breakfast.

Timothy and Cara would realize I left soon, if not already. I resolved to get moving. With the sack slung over my shoulder and knife at my side, I set out.

The morning was brisk and fog clouded the woods. I stepped lightly watching for depressions that might be a trap. Soon, the fog appeared thicker ahead. When I reached it, the smell of smoke became strong.

I pulled the extra shirt from my bag and wrapped it around my face. I traveled from tree to tree and listened for people. When there is smoke, there is fire, I remembered. Out here, fire meant people. My senses were on full alert.

A scream broke through the trees. Birds scattered from their roosts above me. I crouched at the base of the nearest pine. When no cry followed, I crept forward. Sweat beaded on my forehead.

Another blood curdling scream rang out from ahead. It was a woman's voice, it stabbed through my temples. Again, she wailed, louder than I thought humanly possible.

I ran toward the deafening sound. It muffled any noise I made. The scream lasted longer than the others had. It gave me time to scurry into an alcove made by a fallen tree and its roots.

I could hear shouts, a hundred feet, or so, away from my hiding place. The cries belonged to more than one person, I distinguished them now. Ash and voices floated in the breeze from their direction.

I peered through the tangled roots that protruded from the earth. A blaze enveloped a tree's base. Four people were positioned strategically around its perimeter.

They wore black military gear, helmets, body armor, and tall boots. They each had a high-power rifle pointed up into the branches. My eyes rose to where they pointed, at a treehouse.

My breath lodged in my chest. It was our treehouse. I had walked in circles during the night. Growing up, I heard stories about people getting lost in the woods because they walked in circles, unaware of direction. This was where I started. It came crashing down upon me that Cara and Timothy were up there.

"Traitors!" One of the soldiers yelled. "Come down here or burn; it makes no difference to us!"

I sank to my knees. What was I going to do? They had betrayed me, lied to me. Could I allow them to burn alive? Could I live with myself if I didn't try to save them?

My heart raced; my decision was made before I had more time to think. I lifted myself to take a better look. I couldn't see Cara or Timothy, maybe one of them made it out.

Then Cara screamed and Timothy emerged onto the small landing by the trunk. I felt like the Roar hit me. My breath was knocked out of me; my knees were weak. I saw movement behind him and knew Cara was trapped too.

It was up to me to save them. I scanned the floor for something to create a diversion. There was a pile of rocks nearby. I shoved them closer to my hiding place. I picked one up and turned to the stand-off.

"You two turned from us. You both know the world can't survive with those monsters running the surface any longer. Why fight us?" The same soldier called out.

"I can't kill them anymore. You made me, you made me kill people!" Timothy cried. "There is good in some of them and I can't allow all of them to die."

"Timothy, you are an idiot. When did you go soft? You were bred for this!" The soldier yelled. "These humans poisoned the Earth and we will right all of it. You and your sister make no difference."

"Then why are you here? Willing to burn us alive?" Timothy spat.

The flames climbed higher.

I held the rock waiting for the most opportune moment. A part of me also wanted to hear what Timothy had to say.

"You took our girl." The soldier shrugged. "We will still be able to use her, whether she is burned up there or not."

They had to be talking about me. What did that mean?

Timothy yelled. "I would die for her!"

"You may get your wish!" The soldier turned to his comrades. "Light the branches."

Two of them bent down and opened canisters. This was my moment. I threw the rock as far as I could, behind the furthest soldier.

They all turned as I had hoped. "Go check it out." The main soldier ordered.

Two of the men retreated to the tree line. I popped up a second time and threw one at the closest soldier's head. The rock collided with his head. A hollow crack rang out and his legs gave way.

Timothy sprang from the tree and crashed upon the nearest soldier. They both crumpled onto the ground. Timothy was on top and raised the knife plunging it down.

I ran into the opening, to the man I hit. He was unconscious. Timothy and I met eyes as the two others burst through the brush. Timothy pointed his gun and shot the first soldier. The second soldier fired before Timothy did. The bullet missed him.

I charged at the soldier, his eyes wide. He pointed the gun at me and it clicked when he pulled the trigger; it misfired.

I didn't have time to think or absorb the finality of my strike. I just slashed the knife into him. He dropped to the ground. I didn't even look at what I had done. I fell to my knees. Timothy sprinted past me to finish my messy job. The screams stopped.

Cara appeared on the landing. "Timothy!" Her voice cracked.

He ran toward the tree. I forced myself to go to where he stood.

"You have to jump!" He told her.

"I can't, it's too high!" She screamed.

"I'll catch you. Do it!" He demanded.

She looked from him to me and let go of the railing. In midair, she screamed the same way that brought back my memories of the Roar. Timothy caught her and rolled onto the ground. The maneuver dumped them into a heap.

For a moment, we all just breathed. Cara sat up first. She brushed herself off, and cursed.

She stood and gave me a look of hatred. "Did you rat us out?"

I stuttered. "Are-are you serious?"

Timothy interrupted. "Cara, she just saved us."

"Then why in the world was she not with us?" Cara exclaimed.

Anger rose inside of me and poured out.

"Maybe, because I heard your conversation last night." I snarled.

They looked dumbfounded.

"Yeah, I heard about how I don't fit into your plans. I know about your lies and taking me to someone that might hurt me, so I left. Lucky for you, I am apparently a complete idiot at navigation and walked in circles all night or I'd be long gone." I slammed my hands into my pockets.

"You heard us?" Cara asked.

"You tried to leave?" Timothy added.

"Yes and yes." I replied.

Timothy reached for my hand and I snapped it away. "Don't!"

"I'm sorry, Alex." Cara apologized. She sat back down.

"I know we need to explain ourselves but we need to get away from here and fast." Timothy said. "If those guys don't check in soon, they will send reinforcements."

"Tell me why I should go with you?" I was on the verge of tears, which made me even angrier.

"If you were here, then you heard me say I would die for you. I meant it, you are more important both of us. The person that commissioned us thinks you have the key to end this!" Timothy exclaimed.

"I can't digest that right now," I confessed. A few tears rolled down my cheeks.

Cara pointed at the flames. "I guess we don't need anything up there, do we?"

"Not bad enough to risk being burned alive," Timothy said. "Give me a minute to put the bodies in there." He nodded toward the fire.

"Wait, you are going to burn them?" I gawked.

"They are all dead. Burning them might slow down any searches for us. They will try to find out if any of the bodies were us." Timothy pressed his lips together.

The gravity of my part in the deaths of these soldiers crashed down on me. I sputtered and shook. Cara helped me to my feet. I glanced at the body of the soldier I attacked. The body was motionless and a pool of blood outlined his torso. I gagged at what I had done.

"I'm going to get her out of here. Do it quick." Cara commanded.

I limped away from the scene. Cara steadied me. We weaved through the trees. I stumbled along. I heaved a couple more times and produced only my small breakfast. Cara let me take my time but urgency radiated from her.

"It's okay." She soothed, rubbing my back. "The first time you kill is like this, for most. I always remind myself that if I had not killed them they would've gladly killed me."

My face twisted. "They weren't going to kill me. They were going to kill you."

"Don't you think for a second that once they were done with us they wouldn't have hunted you." She snapped.

"That's a terrible thank you." I retorted.

She gave me a wry smile. "Glad to see you still have some wit about you. Thank you."

Timothy ran up from behind. "What's wrong? Why is she limping?" He asked Cara.

She shrugged.

"It's my leg, it started bleeding last night. I didn't do anything to it." I answered for Cara.

"We will have a look when we get to a safer place." He sighed. "Can you run?"

Cara winked at him in response. Timothy hoisted me onto his back. They both broke into a sprint. My head bounced around. I didn't care enough to lay it on his shoulder. They ran effortlessly through the forest. They jumped fallen trees and avoided thickets.

I was sick to my stomach. I killed someone. My mouth watered at the thought and I muffled sobs from escape.

Flashes of the soldier, when my knife made impact came whenever I closed my eyes, so I forced them to stay open. My surroundings and time became a blur.

As expected, Cara became winded first. "I need to rest a little." She panted and slowed.

"I'm going to go a little more and I'll come back for you." Timothy promised.

He pumped his legs. Cara fell behind. I looked back to see the distance grow between us. She had her hands on her knees. She gasped for air.

Timothy ran a mile or so before he broke pace.

"I'm going to leave you here." He propped me against a tree. "I'll be right back, I promise." He put a hand on my head as he spoke.

He tore off to retrieve Cara. I hugged my knees to my chest. I still shook, but had stopped crying. My knife poked me in the back so I pulled it from the straps. I held it in front of me. The blood from the soldier remained on the blade. I tossed it beside me, but couldn't take my eyes from it.

The blood was undoubtedly mole blood, but it was exactly like my own. I don't know if I expected it to be green or something abnormal. Nonetheless, it made no difference in killing a person or a thing.

Tears welled up once more. I sucked in air and reached for the knife. I cleaned it on the bark of the tree. I didn't want the blood to make me think about it anymore.

Chapter Twenty-One

A couple of minutes later, Timothy halted in front of me, Cara on his back. She still breathed heavily. He knelt before me and she slid down and stepped away. His expression was one filled with worry and apologies.

"Can I look at your leg?" Timothy asked. He put his hand on my knee.

I nodded. He rolled back my pant leg to expose the bandage made from cloth. It was soaked with blood.

Cara came closer to get a better look. Timothy untied the bandage and pulled it from the dried scab. I grimaced as it tore away.

The wound itself wasn't very big, the scab only an inch or two in diameter. He inspected the opening while Cara dug in her pockets. She produced a small vile of her salve. Timothy's fingers felt around my scar and pressed upon the raised skin. His brow furrowed in thought.

"This can be fixed for now." He glanced at Cara and took the vile. I noticed her brow was creased just like his.

"What?" I probed.

"Alex, there is something in your leg. I'm not a hundred percent sure but it might be what our client is looking for." Cara remarked.

I retracted from Timothy's touch. I left his hand in midair.

His face was solemn. "I think so, too. I didn't meet with him, but Cara told me that he wanted you because you had something that could stop the killing. I believe it is in your leg."

"I've had this scar longer than I can remember." I recalled.

"Alex, you can't remember how you got it." Cara reasoned. "It may have been implanted during a Roar and you would never know. I've seen them manipulate memories and time."

I panicked. "Well then, what is it?"

"It feels like a capsule or something." Timothy replied. "When I pushed on it, it moves. Does it hurt?"

"Not when you touch it. When I walk, the pain has been getting worse." I whined. "I want it out." I pinched at the spot.

"I can't take it out. I have no idea what it is exactly or if there is something that could damage you if I were to take it." Cara cautioned.

"You mean there might be a booby trap?" I croaked.

"There might be. If I remove it out here, there is the natural chance of infection; there could also be unforeseen complications that were put in to place to keep it from falling into the wrong hands." She revealed. "I will put some of the salve on the scab. I am concerned that your body is trying to push it out. People's bodies will do that with foreign objects, over time."

She dabbed some of the medicine on the wound. Timothy held my hand and rubbed my calf. They both appeared to be genuinely concerned.

"Listen, this is a distraction, but don't think you are off the hook. You both have a lot of explaining to do." I stated.

"We will have time for that when we get to the river." Timothy reckoned.

He swept me into his arms and carried me, with Cara at his side. His strides were long and even. Despite everything, I felt safe there in his arms. If this thing in my leg could stop people from dying, we had to get to the coast.

The glimmer of hope that someone I knew waited for me diminished altogether. My heart tightened at the thought. I held Timothy's jacket in my fist. I needed to be comforted.

He bowed his head to me in his arms. "We will get through this." He reassured me. His black eyes pierced through mine.

Timothy had said on more than one occasion that he would make sure I made it. I had proof that he needed me, but did he want me? I pushed that out of my mind. It was illogical and a waste of time. I needed to survive; nothing else mattered.

"I'm scared." I admitted.

"I am too." He confessed.

"Me too." Cara chimed in. "If we weren't I'd question our sanity." She picked a leaf from a tree and dissected it.

"Tell me something good." I muttered to them.

"Oh, wait until you see the ocean. When I saw it for the first time, it brought me to tears." Cara sang. "I never knew it would be so beautiful, so immense."

Timothy chuckled, "Cara wouldn't leave the beach that first day. She ran along the shore like a child. I loved it too, running the sand between my toes. It was nothing like anything I had experienced." He shook his head. "We were both sunburned beyond belief. Our skin eventually got used to the sun, but I'll never forget that pain."

"My skin blistered. I thought it was going to shed down to my bones." She reminisced. "Thank goodness, there were UV lights underground or I'm sure I would have died from sun poisoning. It was worth it though. I'd never been happier than that first day at the beach."

I recalled my own trips to the ocean. My family played in the sand, collected shells at the water's edge, and the warmth of the sun upon my skin. I'd even liked the way the salt clung to everything; the taste of it on my mouth. I wanted to be there with all my heart.

Deep in those memories we continued in silence. I wondered if we could have a day like that together when we arrived. It would be heaven on earth to put everything behind me and just enjoy life for a day.

We made good ground and stopped to rest beside a creek. I had the baggy of dried meat to share for lunch. Timothy refilled our water bladders and massaged his arms from carrying me. I insisted that I felt better and would walk from here. I hated being a burden.

I splashed cold water from the creek on my face. It stung my face and hands. I lay flat to watch the tree limbs sway in the breeze above.

The sound of the nettles rustled and calmed me.

Timothy was the first to get antsy. He wanted to get to the river by nightfall. So, amid groans from Cara and I, we started moving.

I limped along in the beginning. Timothy became concerned and I brushed him off. I sucked up the nagging ache to walk as normal as possible.

We rounded a corner to find a community left abandoned from the end of the world. It was the first time I had seen what our civilization had become. The houses were large and built of brick. The roofs sagged from years left unattended. Most of them were overgrown by kudzu or other vines. Cars were strewn about in the road. They rusted in the elements.

Timothy snagged me behind a tree. "Usually I avoid going near any remnants of your world like this. We need to cut close because the river is just past the hills on the other side. There is nothing there for us; do you understand?"

My eyes were wide at the sight of the ruins. "I didn't know anything had made it through."

He nodded. "Places like this are out there, but there may be inhabitants. Be quiet and stay hidden."

"What if one of these cars could still run? It might make traveling faster."

"The Roar took all transportation remember? Some places stand only because of their distance from the machines. It still wiped out all electronics and engines. There is nothing of use to us here. It has been ransacked by our people and they took what could be used." He took off his jacket and stuffed it into the bag.

I closed my eyes. I didn't think I'd ever see a house or cars again. The urge to investigate subsided. If this made Timothy nervous it had to be worth listening to him.

Cara took the lead. Timothy kept an eye on the houses as he moved from shadow to tree. I trailed behind him.

Chapter Twenty-Two

I saw a curtain in one of the house windows sway. I paused and motioned for them to do the same. I held my breath as I peeked around the tree. It may have been the wind blowing through a shattered window. I waved at them to proceed.

"Who's there?" A voice called. A shotgun cocked.

Cara glared at me. Timothy shook his head with his finger on his lips to quiet us. I lowered myself to a squat. There were bushes that I could look through without being seen.

A man stood on a deck of one of the houses. He held a shotgun pointed in our direction.

"I will shoot you dead if you come any closer, I swear!" He yelled.

Timothy looked weary. He raised his hands and stepped out from behind the tree. He kept his head low, to hide his eyes.

"Sir, we're just passing by. I'm sorry if we alarmed you, but I promise we aren't looking for trouble!" He shouted.

"Yeah, I heard that before." The man accused.

"Sir, we are going to the river. We don't mean any harm." Timothy called.

"How many of you are there?" The man lowered his gun.

"Only three of us, me and two girls." Timothy announced.

"Are you armed?" The man yelled.

"Only to protect ourselves." Timothy stated.

"Make your people come out. I want to see them." The man waved to the door and a guy about our age came onto the deck with a gun aimed at Timothy.

Timothy took a chance and motioned for us to join him. "Both of you stay behind me."

Cara and I approached Timothy. We stayed in his shadow. The man relaxed in his stance. He and the boy talked in hushed voices.

They came to an agreement of what to do with us. "You told the truth about your companions being girls. I suppose you probably told the truth about your weapons. I'm going to allow you to pass, but we will have our sights on you at all times. My son and I won't hesitate to kill you if you try anything." He hollered.

Timothy made sure to put himself between the house, Cara, and me. His hand brushed mine and I slipped my fingers around his. I took Cara's hand in my other and we walked past the houses. I was sure that the guns were still pointed at our backs; it seemed that Timothy had made the right choice to reveal us to them.

Soon, the road lay before us. I let go of them. Our boots clanked upon the concrete. My eyes continued to scan the houses for more movement.

"Hey, wait up." Someone called out behind us. The young man ran toward us.

I wielded my knife around. Timothy pulled Cara's knife. It was the boy. He trotted along the road, his hands raised in peace. His gun was holstered. I brought the knife to my side. Timothy and Cara lowered their heads, to not give away that they were moles.

"Wait, please. I haven't seen anyone else but my Dad and our people in so long," he sounded desperate, "at least no one that wasn't trying to kill us."

"How do you know we won't try to kill you?" Timothy growled his head still low, the knife at his side.

“You had on a red jacket, right? It means you are friendly, plus you were going away like my dad asked.” He reasoned.

He kept his hands raised. He was cute in a boyish way. His blonde hair long and messy; stubble grew from his chin. His eyes were noteworthy though, they were sparkling blue. They had innocence in them I hadn’t seen in forever.

“The red jacket didn’t keep you two from threatening us.” Timothy retorted.

“We have to be careful. You know how people are out here, man.” The guy lifted a shoulder. “My name is Max.” He held a hand out to me.

I took a step forward and took his hand. Timothy and Cara tensed protectively. Max shook my hand.

I blubbered. “Nice to meet you. I’m very sorry but we have to get going.”

“Max, is everything alright?” His dad called from an open window.

“Yeah dad, it’s fine.” Max huffed. “I get the overprotective thing, too.” He winked.

“We’ve had a rough time, too.” I understood. “My friends have been on the road a long time.”

“My dad and I were separated in the beginning. He found me though and we’ve been lucky to lay low.” He said sympathetically.

Cara grew impatient. "What do you want?"

Max swayed from her boldness. "Ok, I'll cut the crap; my sister is sick. I wanted to ask if you guys have any medicine or something that might help her. We found pain killers in a medicine cabinet but that only helps with the pain. I think she needs antibiotics."

I looked back at Cara and Timothy. They talked under their breaths. Max wrung his hands in anticipation.

"Please, I can't stand to see her like this. I know you don't fully trust me. I understand, but if you will show me you have meds, I'll give you my gun." He begged.

"Hold on." I backed up to Timothy and Cara. "You have to help." I insisted. "If he will give you his gun, I think we would be ok."

Cara eyed me. "How do we know they won't kill us as soon as he sees what we are?"

"I'll handle that part." I decided.

They both stared at each other a moment and nodded. "If he makes one move, I'm shooting them and we are getting out of here," Timothy announced.

I went back to Max. "We will help, but I have to tell you something first." I said gently. "You have to promise me that you will hear me out and if you can't deal with it, we walk."

He smiled broadly. "Anything, heck, I'll even throw in dinner and a warm place to stay if you will help her."

"My friends are not like you and me." I started. "They saved me from the moles. They have been protecting me and guiding me to someone that can stop all of this. Cara and Timothy are like them."

His mouth dropped. He eyes darted to each of us.

"Calm down." I raised my hand. "They can help your sister. I have been shot and I swear I was healed in hours." I pushed back my sleeve to reveal the white mark that was left. "See?"

He closed his mouth and moved to inspect the scar further. "They saved you?"

"Yes, a man sliced my back and Timothy's arm. We both would have died, but Cara healed us. She knows what to do." I reassured him.

Max stared at our little group in amazement. "I'll be darned; two dirt devils saved a human."

"That's what we do." Cara shrugged.

Max laughed. "I guess it doesn't matter who saves my little sister, but the old man might have some hang ups. Give me a few minutes to talk to him."

"You got five minutes then we leave." Timothy warned.

Max ran toward the house. We all stood in the road and waited.

"What have we gotten ourselves into now?" Timothy complained.

"Listen, like Cara said, this is what you do. Hopefully, we will get to warm up a bit and have a decent meal." I persuaded them. "This girl might die if you don't do something."

Timothy crossed his arms over his chest. He was not happy with our involvement with these people.

Cara gulped. "Besides, Max is kind of cute."

"Of course, you girls want to help him because he's kind of cute." Timothy rebuked.

"Timothy, be nice." I glared at him.

"What? I've dealt with you two lovebirds this whole way. Get over it." Cara added.

Max reappeared from the house. He trotted toward us. "My dad isn't too happy about it, but he will keep himself together to save his baby girl. She needs help badly and he knows it."

Timothy lifted his head, exposing his eyes. "Is he going to be able to handle seeing this?" Timothy regarded him.

“Wow.” Max retracted. “That is a little startling.” Max looked me in the face. “I had no idea.”

“You’ve never seen one of us?” Cara wondered.

“No, but it doesn’t matter, like I said. What does matter is that your friend doesn’t seem to want to be bothered with this.” Max responded.

“He will be ok. He’s just got his feathers ruffled because Cara told him you are cute.” I chuckled.

Both he and Cara blushed. “Kind of, I said. Kind of cute.” She corrected.

Max smirked. “I’ll take that as a compliment even from a dirt dweller.”

“Okay, okay, Cara, show him the vials of medicine so I can have the gun.” Timothy instructed.

Cara opened the bag to show the few bottles she had stuffed in her pockets before she jumped from the treehouse. The glance was enough for Max. He disarmed and handed the gun to Timothy.

Timothy checked the chamber and magazine. It was fully loaded. Timothy approved the barter.

Cara took her place next to Max. She touched his arm and told him his sister would be okay. Max smiled at her in appreciation.

Timothy groaned. I took his arm and we walked toward the house. He gave me a nasty look or two as Cara probed about what was wrong with the sister. I caught snippets of their chatter. His sister had a hacking, wet cough and a high fever.

The Tylenol Max scavenged had helped to keep the fever down, but her coughing, aches, and sweats had rendered her bedbound. He was worried to the extent that he sounded frantic.

The brick steps to the front door rocked under our feet. Max entered first. The foyer set a solemn tone to our visit. It welcomed us with a dingy and dull aura.

Cautiously, I stepped inside with Timothy. A living room lay before us. Max waved us inside further. A few huddled bodies were cast about the room. A couple of them belonged to young girls and boys wrapped in blankets, their eyes peeped from them. An old man and woman lay bundled on the couch.

"Max?" I paused. "Why didn't you tell us there were more people in here?"

"I was afraid you wouldn't come." He confessed. "None of them are able bodied or can fight. We take care of them."

I shook my head at him. "If you want to be trusted, you cannot lie through omission."

Timothy pulled me back to the door. "I'm done here."

"Wait! I promise none of them can hurt you. Most of them we found here in the houses starving or unable to survive on their own." Max panicked.

Timothy relented once he noticed the hopeless eyes that peered at him from the corners of the room. He looked at my face and saw my silent plead. Timothy's grip loosened.

A deep ragged cough echoed from upstairs. Cara turned her head to a stairway to the right of the living room.

"Is that your sister?" She asked.

"Yes. Please forgive me. I needed you to see what state we are living in. We are trying to save people too. If I told you there were ten people in the house would you have come?"

"Where's your father?" Timothy demanded. "Upstairs with Lily. He won't let you work on her if he isn't there. He needs to see what you are doing. Can you blame him?" Max defended.

"I guess not." Cara agreed. "Take me to her."

"Is he armed?" Timothy questioned. "I don't want any more surprises."

"He is, but so are you. You outnumber us. It would be stupid of him to try anything." Max pointed out.

We timidly followed Max. The stairs creaked loudly as we climbed them.

Lily coughed several more times. Her effort made me wince. Timothy had his hand on the gun at his side, ready for any trick. I held his other hand and caressed his knuckles with my fingers to soothe his nerves.

We rounded a doorway to find his sister laid on a bed covered in sheets. She was so small and meek, maybe four years old. Her hair was the same as his, the color of straw, but it stuck to her forehead from sweat. Her eyes were the same blue, but clouded and pink in the whites.

His sister sat up and hacked into a cloth her father held over her face. Max's dad had thick creases between his eyebrows from concern. He patted Lily on the back and rubbed her shoulders. Lily's skin was a sickly color of gray.

Cara looked over her shoulder at me, eyes wide. I knew Lily was in bad shape. I didn't need Cara to tell me.

"How long has she been like this?" Cara directed to Max.

"She's been coughing for a month, now. We have been fighting the fever for a couple of weeks." He revealed.

Max's father stood when he saw us. He appeared to be sizing us up.

Cara introduced herself. “My name is Cara. I am going to see if there is anything I can do to help.”

Cara moved quickly to Lily’s side. She laid her head on Lily’s chest. She listened intently. Her face fell and turned white. I knew the prognosis wasn’t good.

Max’s dad moved toward us. He hadn’t looked so big at a distance. I noticed the rag in his hand was covered with thick dark blood. His expression was lost. His eyes were exhausted and swollen from sorrow.

Cara hugged Lily and backed away. “I need to talk to you in the hall.” She herded us out of the room.

“This is beyond my medicine.” Cara croaked. “She has clots in her lungs.” Her eyes welled with tears.

“How can you tell? You only listened for a second.” Max asked softly.

Cara reached for him. “I can hear the rumbling in her lungs when she breathes, her heart is faint, and I can hear the effort of her blood pushing past the valves.” Cara trembled. “It’s possible she has tuberculosis.”

“She’s not going to die.” Max’s father shoved Cara. She bounced off the wall and slid down on her back.

Timothy restrained him. "Get him under control, Max."

Cara softly said. "I'm so sorry, if I had been here sooner-."

Max faced me and searched for truth in my eyes. I bowed my head.

His lip quivered. "Dad, we knew this was coming. She has been sick for so long and it has been bad." He gripped his father's arms.

Max's dad slumped to the floor. He obviously knew that Cara was right. He thumped his head on the carpeted floor and wept. Timothy let him go.

Max went back to his sister. He enveloped her in his arms and rocked her. She whined and snuggled into him.

A tear rolled down my cheek for the little girl and her family. At least Lily would find peace soon. Death was always hard on the people it left behind.

Chapter Twenty-Three

Cara crawled toward Max's dad. She stroked his back to try to console him.

He shot up and growled. "Why? Why did you do this?"

"Our people did this, not us." She said evenly. "My brother and I don't believe in any of this."

"Their mother died giving birth to her. They took her from me. If she had been in a hospital, she would be alive. Instead, I had to watch her slowly die from losing blood. Now, I must watch my baby girl die, too." He sobbed.

Tears rolled out of all our eyes.

Cara sniffled. "I am so sorry. I would gladly kill them all for doing this. It isn't right to let people suffer, especially little ones like her."

He placed his head in his hands and cried. In Lily's room, Max hummed for his sister to drown out our conversation.

His sister stuttered painfully. "Max did I die?"

"No baby. Why?" He ran his fingers through her hair.

"The girl that hugged me had black eyes. I thought she was here to take me." Lily wheezed.

She went into another coughing fit. This time blood splattered onto her chest. She began to cry at the sight of it.

Cara shrank against the wall. "It might be better for her not to see me again. I do have something that will help her to sleep."

The fathered nodded and waited for Cara to remove the bottle from the bag. She handed the whole thing to him.

"Give her two drops at a time. It will make her sleep for at least four hours at a time. I suggest saving some until the end. When you are ready to say goodbye, give her ten drops. She will quietly slip away." Cara instructed.

His eyes were so distant at the thought. "I can't- I can't do that."

"Yes, you can." Timothy urged. "She is your daughter and you won't want her to suffer through what is coming."

He clutched the bottle in his hands. He nodded slowly. I watched his gaze flit to the gun at his side.

Timothy placed his hand on the father's back. "You have to be strong. You must take care of them. There are people here that need you."

"Thank you." Max's dad mumbled.

He picked up his gun and dragged his feet to the room with Lily and Max. Max handed Lily to his father and came back out to us.

"Thank you for-," he paused. "I appreciate you coming."

His eyes flooded and I hugged him. "I'm so sorry." I repeated.

Timothy put his hand on my shoulder to cut the embrace short. "I apologize, Max, but we really should be going. We should give your family space."

I shot him a dirty look. He avoided my eyes, but took my hand.

Max offered. "But, I promised you a meal?"

"We really appreciate that but the day is fading and we need to make time on the road." He pulled me toward the stairs.

We all hurried down the stairs. Cara hugged Max and whispered something in his ear. He choked up and a few tears escaped his eyes.

Timothy rushed us out the door. He took both of our hands and walked quickly away from the house. I had to trot to keep up with his strides.

"Timothy, what is going on?" I huffed.

He answered me with silence until we made it to the tree line across the road. "Have you been inoculated?" He asked. He started tugging on my sleeve. "Tell me you were as a child." His face was stricken with fear.

"Yes, I think so. I had all of the normal shots they give you." I panicked a little. "My mom was religious about taking us for them and to checkups. Why?"

Timothy dropped his arms at his sides and sighed in relief. Cara was beside herself. Neither she, nor I had thought of the danger I was in, if I hadn't been vaccinated.

A gunshot rang out. We all froze. Then another followed, screams carried from the house, another and another came. The hairs on my neck stood out, more shots fired.

Timothy shoved past me. "Cara, keep her here!" He exclaimed. He took off toward the house.

I leapt to follow him, but Cara yanked me back. The shots continued.

Timothy ran faster than I had ever seen. He landed on the front step when Max fell out of the door covered in blood. Timothy grabbed him and lifted him onto the door frame. He yelled at Max.

Max hung his head and vomited to the side. Timothy dropped him into the bushes and sprang into the house. Max was tangled in the bushes. Cara and I heard him wail.

"Cara, let go of me!" I demanded.

She let go and I hit the ground at a sprint. She wasn't far behind. Max continued to scream as we reached him, with his bottom half caught above him in the holly bush. He cursed as he cried, but didn't move.

Cara crouched by his head. "What happened? Tell me!" She screamed over him.

"He did it! He killed them all!" Max bleated.

I pushed the front door open and pulled my knife out of my belt. "Timothy!" I yelled.

"Wait!" Cara reached for me. I sidestepped her and slipped through the entrance.

"Timothy!" I called again.

The couches in front on me dripped blood. I walked further into the living room. Bodies lay strewn across the floor each with puddles of red that outlined them. I took in the scene; none of the bodies moved.

Footsteps pounded upon the stairs. I turned and Timothy was at my side. I looked back at the massacre.

At the edge of my eye, I saw him curl over. His hands rested on his knees.

"He did it. He killed them all. He gave Lily half the bottle." Timothy panted. He opened his clenched hand with what was left of the medicine. "He killed himself."

"I can't process this." I struggled. It seemed like a nightmare.

Timothy turned angry and he seethed. "I told Cara to keep you out. Where is she?"

"Outside with Max." I whispered.

Timothy wrapped his arms around me and walked me out the front door. I leaned against Timothy for support. My legs felt numb.

Cara sat in the yard with Max on his hands and knees. He dry-heaved over and over.

"Why? Why?" He repeated.

I dug my nails into Timothy's arm. We looked upon the mess that had been left by his father. How could I make this excusable? A father is supposed to be strong. He is supposed to take care of you.

Timothy squeezed my hand. "I can't imagine." He breathed, as though he read my mind.

I forgot that they never knew their fathers. I remembered mine as steadfast and caring. He would never leave me with a burden like this if given any other option.

Visions of my own father flickered in my head. The flashbacks were ghosts of him. He showed me how to fix things, pushed me to be better, and protected me from myself. I folded in on myself and dropped to the ground where Max and Cara were.

The three of us sobbed. Timothy joined us and held me to him. What Max's father did was incomprehensible.

Cara probed his body as he writhed. "Were you shot?"

Max moaned as she felt his body looking for a wound. It was hard to tell, there was so much blood on him.

"Is he dead?" He finally groaned.

Cara held his face in her hands and nodded. Max sobbed loudly. "Did he kill her?"

Cara turned to Timothy. He closed his eyes.

She held him around the waist. "He did it peacefully."

Max's eyes rolled into the back of his head. Thankfully, he didn't faint.

"There has been too much noise here." Timothy interrupted. "I hate to be this way but Max needs to decide whether he is coming with us or staying?"

Cara gave Max the choice. She quickly told him that she would protect him if he came, but if he stayed there was no telling who might have heard the screams or the gunshots. If he stayed, he would be alone to fend for himself.

Max gathered himself for a moment; he closed his eyes and thought. We all held our breath.

He sat up upon his knees. "I have to go. I will be stronger than he was." I saw a spark of anger behind his eyes.

Cara and Timothy helped him to his feet. Max quietly cried from there. He knew that was part of the bargain. He had to stay quiet. Cara let him lean on her for support but we walked quickly from the house.

There was no reason to stay there any longer.

The trees enveloped us and it felt safer. Timothy paused briefly to ask Max if he had vaccinations when he was young. Max told us that his father told him he had the TB vaccine before he went on his massacre.

His father told him to get out of the house, but he refused and when his dad started shooting, he tried to tackle him. His father was too big and threw him. Max told us he was thrown onto the living room floor which was why he was covered in blood. All the other's blood splattered on him. He thought his dad was going to shoot him, but he ran upstairs to die with his baby girl.

The whole story made me weak and distraught. I didn't know how to help him or even give him a glimmer of hope from the abyss his father had made.

His whole body trembled; his knees wobbled. Timothy caught him just as he fainted. Timothy laid him down, gently.

Cara sat and placed his head in her lap. "What are we going to do? We can't leave him here." She eyed Timothy for his approval.

Timothy ran both his hands through his dark hair. He stared at the sky. "If he can't walk, I guess I'll have to carry him." Timothy concluded.

"Give me a second." Cara turned.

Cara caressed Max's face and said his name in a whisper. She coaxed him to wake. Soon, he moaned and his eyes opened.

He looked at Cara for a moment. "I can see why Lily thought you were an angel coming to take her."

She smiled back and rubbed his shoulders.

"I need you to be able to function." Timothy broke in. "There is a good chance that people of our kind will be coming to investigate. I know you have been through a lot so if you don't think you can, I am going to have to carry you."

Max closed his eyes and sighed.

"I think you can do this." Cara said.

"I think you can, too." I added.

"I will get myself together." He stated. "I keep thinking that I want to make sure they are all buried properly, but I couldn't do it on my own."

A single tear rolled out of the corner of his eye.

"No one can blame you for that thought. They were your family." Timothy affirmed.

"Will you help me up?" Max raised an arm. Timothy pulled him to his feet. Max nodded. "I guess we better get going, then."

Cara draped Max's arm over her and held his hand. "Let's go." She motioned ahead.

We all forged ahead. Max stumbled along with Cara, but she kept him at pace. Timothy placed me under his arm in a protective manner. We climbed a steep hill and finally saw the river in the distance.

We paused at the crest of the hill to drink. Timothy proposed that we make our way to the river bank and hold up for the night. The rest of us nodded or grunted in agreement. The light got dim so stopping would be necessary soon.

Something dawned on me as we walked. Max didn't have the special boots we did.

"Timothy." I slowed so that Cara and Max would be a little in front of us. "What about Max not having boots like ours?"

His eyes widened. "Honestly, I hadn't thought about it. What an idiot!" He cursed himself. "We will have back track some, to throw off our path. I need Cara and you to find some metal quickly."

"Cara!" I called. "We have a problem."

They hobbled to us. Timothy explained the situation. Both of their eyes widened at the thought of us being tracked.

"I bet that is how they found us at the treehouse. We got too comfortable and took our shoes off at the shore of the pond." Cara guessed.

The three of us slumped. What a stupid mistake.

Timothy immediately grabbed Max's shoulder.

"We will meet you at the river's edge. Max, it doesn't look like you are going to have much of a choice, at some point you are going for a ride."

He pointed to a spot a little to the east. "You have to find me some metal to cover the bottom of his shoes." Timothy demanded. "Meet us there."

"Timothy, where am I going to find metal out here?" Cara whined.

He opened his mouth to say something unpleasant, so I interrupted. "We will make it work."

I pulled her down the hill. When I looked back, Timothy and Max were gone.

"Seriously, Alex, where are we going to find metal?" Cara questioned. She tugged at me to stop.

"Does it have to be a certain type?" I asked.

"The thicker the better for wear and tear, but as a temporary fix, no." She said.

"Good, that gives us a better chance. A tin can or aluminum will do for now. Once we get to the boat, it won't matter, right?" I confirmed.

She nodded in agreement.

I directed us straight down the hill. We might have a better opportunity to find human trash washed ashore that we could use.

I kept an eye down while I listened to the sounds around us. Everything was still. I didn't even hear birds or squirrels. I held my finger to my lips. If it was this quiet, it wouldn't take much for us to be heard.

Our feet slipped a couple of times and we clung to each other and trees for support. The leaves that were among the decline were slippery from decay.

At the bottom of the hill, the ground leveled. I let out a breath of relief. A fall out here could set us back even more.

Once the sun fully set, Cara stopped and pulled a small case from her pocket. She plucked the contacts from her eyes and placed them back into her pants. She gestured that it would help her to see more clearly.

A few steps further, she held her hand up for me to stop. She tilted her head from side to side to her right. She pranced over to a muddy spot and brushed some leaves aside. She returned to me with an empty soda can. We both grinned at her treasure. We just needed one more piece.

Soon, the sound of the river became audible. It started as a thin white noise, but as we approached, it turned into an ominous rumble. The current was strong, the water brown, careened over and through rocks jutting from the bottom.

I searched the bushes and shore line for trash. I found a plastic bag plastered against a tree trunk. I shook it out. There were no holes, so I stuffed it in our knapsack. We walked further east and did a sweep for anything that glinted among the muck.

Cara waved me over to the river. She pointed to the middle, where a log laid across a rock. Stuck between them was a can.

I nodded. "I'll get it."

She shook her head. "No, Alex, Timothy will kill me if you get hurt."

That made me want to be the one to get it even more. "Don't be silly." I shrugged.

I stepped off the river bed before she could argue and balanced on the closest rock. She grimaced at me and put her hands on her hips. I tested the next rock and hopped over.

I looked ahead. Two more rocks and I would be there. I swayed a bit, but steadied with my arms out straight. I kept them out as I stepped onto the next rock.

The last one was wet and dark. It made me a little nervous. I stuck a leg out and probed the surface. It was going to be a tough one because it was very slick.

I tried to shift my weight to the last rock before launched myself from the one I balanced. My foot slid off the surface and into the water. The rest of me followed. My side skidded along the jagged rock as I fell.

Cara gasped and stepped into the river. I emerged and grasped the rock.

"No, stop. Cara, I'm alright." I sputtered.

She backed up to the shore. "You sure?"

I nodded, still mostly submerged. The current pushed me against the rock. My side burned but was tolerable. The cold water took my breath away. I was already in the water and so close; I decided to go for the dumb can. I clawed my way over to the log and pried the can free. I spit water from my mouth and wiped my eyes. I swam back to the river bed.

I stood dripping wet and shivered uncontrollably, but I had the second can Max needed.

Cara hugged me then pushed me away. "You are a clumsy idiot!" She exclaimed. "I am so mad at you!" A smile broke her frown. "But thank you."

I wrung out my hair. Timothy appeared from the tree line a few yards away. Max was on his back.

"Do I even want to know?" Timothy grumbled.

"Probably not, but we have two cans for Max." I offered.

He raised an eyebrow. "What is that?"

He pointed at my side. Blood had soaked through my shirt. He placed Max on a stump and hurried to me. I shook from the cold and fear of what lie beneath my shirt. Timothy lifted the shirt and exposed a jagged cut. He squatted next to me to inspect it. "I leave you two alone for half an hour."

Cara rummaged around in our belongings for her healing salve. "You guys are really putting me to the test. I'm glad I grabbed this stuff from the treehouse."

"I'm sorry, Timothy. I'm sorry," I repeated.

He looked up at me, worry in his face. "Stop. There is enough out here willing to kill you. I don't need you doing it for them."

"Is it bad?" I asked. I didn't want to look again. The sight of my own blood on my shirt made me woozy.

Cara produced the small bottle and held it to her eyes. "There's not much left," she said.

"Well, let me put it this way, it's not good." He announced and poked the area around the wound.

I flinched, the pressure stung.

I smacked his hand. "It's not like I did it on purpose. Give me a break." I argued.

"With this little bit left, I should stitch you up, then use a tiny bit of the cream. I don't want to run out. We should make camp very soon that way we can get Max's shoes settled and you stitched up."

Max was still waiting on the stump. "And I can help. Right now, I feel like a metaphorical bump on a log."

We all chuckled. He looked so sad but his words were trying to get him through the pain.

Timothy picked me up. "Put pressure on it," he said to me. "I'm going to take Alex down to the platform for camp. I'll be right back. Keep an eye on my sister, Max."

He grinned. "I intend to, don't you worry."

Timothy rolled his eyes. "Exactly what I thought you'd say."

I nudged him.

With large strides, he carried me downriver. He didn't run this time.

"Really, I am sorry. I was just trying to help." I mumbled.

"I know, but I can't stand seeing you hurt." He revealed.

I snuggled into him. "It's going to be okay, right?"

"Yes," he confirmed, "although, it's going to hurt bad when she stitches you up." He winced.

"I can't wait." I rolled my eyes.

He came to a place on the shore where the brush thickened all the way down to the water. He made his way up and through the trees.

On the other side, the rocks were much more prevalent. This seemed like a good place for a shelter to be in the trees. Anyone that came from upriver would be forced to go around the brush. From that direction, yards of rock and a steep embankment would cause a slow and tedious venture.

One of the trees had a vine that hung from it. Timothy pulled it and it unfurled into a knotted ladder.

"You are going to have to move to my back and hold on tight. I know it's going to hurt." He sympathized.

I shifted onto his back. I groaned through the pain. My side throbbed.

Timothy clutched the vine tightly and used his legs to push up. He then slid his hands up further and repeated the motion. Finally, we reached the small platform in the tree. Timothy shrugged me to the side and laid me down. He took off his jacket and tucked it around me.

"Stay put." He kissed me on the cheek and disappeared down the vine.

I stared at the stars above. I could barely hear him make a sound as he hit the ground or headed back to the others. I kept my hands on the wound and shivered. My hands were wet with river water and blood. The thought of being stitched gave me goosebumps.

I heard the vine tighten and Timothy stepped onto the boards. Cara slid from his back. She put her hands on his shoulders.

"Knock it off!" She exclaimed. "I've had to put up with you two lovebirds for a while. Get over it. You better go get him and bring him back safely. Plus, I was just consoling him."

Timothy held his hands in the air. "I'm not sure how you expected me to handle walking up on you in an intimate embrace with someone we know very little about."

"Bleeding here." I interrupted.

They both turned to me.

"I'm serious Timothy, you better not harm a hair on his head." Cara put the vine in his hand. "Go!"

He huffed, but climbed down the vine. Cara spun on her heels and cursed. She tossed the bag beside me, sitting cross-legged.

I whistled. "Seems like that went over well."

She glared at me with her white eyes. "It's ridiculous. He can swoon over you anytime he wants. The moment I like a boy, he freaks."

"First world problems." I chortled.

"What?" She gaped.

"It's something we used to say when something trivial bothered us." I explained.

She frowned at me.

"I just meant that Timothy is upset about a hug that shouldn't matter to him, in the scheme of things." "He definitely has worse to be thinking about." She confirmed.

Cara started to prepare for the procedure. She set a bottle on the floor and pulled a string from her pant leg. Then, she crawled on the boards and picked at splinters.

"Wait." I stopped her. "Are you planning on stitching me with a splinter and a string from your pants?"

"Yes, ma'am, I do." She responded from all fours. "The salve will disinfect the area to make sure it won't give you an infection."

"That sounds perfectly logical." I laughed and rested my head back on the floor.

"Aha!" She exclaimed and pried a sliver from a piece of wood. "Now, I need one to drill a hole through it."

I sighed. The procedure began to resemble torture.

Cara continued to crawl around the platform. The ladder cinched against the tree. Timothy scooted up, Max clung to him. They panted.

"What's wrong?" I asked. My head rested to the side.

Max awkwardly stumbled off Timothy. "Something is on fire." He reported. "It might be my house."

Someone must have heard the gun shots and went to investigate. If someone found a house full of death, it would make sense to set it on fire. Problem was that may draw more attention.

"What do you think?" I asked Timothy.

He made his way to me. He bowed his head and brought my hand to his cheek.

"The smoke was coming from that direction. It very well might be the house." He sighed. "There's not much we can do tonight but stay as quiet as possible to not give away our position. I really hope our backtracking will pay off."

I closed my eyes. The house had been built on the side of a downgrade. The part we were in was above ground level. They couldn't trace the people inside. However, if someone heard the shots and went there, they could have been followed. There were many, what ifs.

Cara swiftly knocked the splinter that was meant to be a needle. She silently pulled Timothy closer. Max took off his shirt and twisted it to make a gag for me. I gave him a mental brownie point for that.

Timothy straddled me and held my hands to his chest. I mentally prepared for the pain to come. Cara poked through my skin.

I wailed into the cloth while Max held it in my mouth. She withdrew the make shift needle and plunged it into my flesh again. I convulsed from the seething pain. This went on, again and again until I thankfully lost consciousness.

Chapter Twenty-Four

Sometime during the night, I awoke to find I was wrapped up in Timothy. He enveloped my body to protect me. I ached, but felt better than I had. I slowly peeled his arm from me and sat upright.

Cara and Max were on the other side of him. They breathed evenly. Max's arm was draped across Cara's stomach. I smiled to myself. I was glad she had found someone to care for.

I lay back down. My breath hung in the air above me in little white puffs. I pulled Timothy's arm back over me and snuggled into his warmth.

As my eyes began to close, a twig cracked from the side of us where the brush thickened. I honed in on the area it originated. Another rustle followed.

I tapped Timothy, his eyes sprang open. My finger on his lip, he waited. A footstep shuffled below.

Timothy motioned for me to stay quiet and not to wake the others. He then turned himself to the space between the boards, his hands held him on a plank. He turned his head to me, sullen.

I bent to look for myself. Between the wood and limbs, a mole soldier crept with a gun pointed ahead.

Two others loomed behind. They scanned the landscape below.

My head shot to the vine. Luckily, someone had remembered to pull it up. The soldier in lead looked up. I held my breath. I hoped the moss and foliage hid us well. He waved the others ahead.

The soldiers passed us and went to the rocks. One of them whispered. I couldn't hear what he said but they turned back. This time, they rounded further into the woods. Timothy placed his hand on my back and pushed me against the floor. A light flashed in the top of the trees behind us. Birds scattered from their roost.

The footsteps trailed off in the distance.

Timothy pulled me close to him. "I am not going to lie to you. I am afraid. If we die out here, I want you to know that I love you. I don't know how it happened, but I do."

His eyes pierced mine. I laid my head sideways on my folded hands.

"I am doing my very best to not fall for you." I admitted. "I know I wasn't part of the plan. If I love you, it will change the things you imagined for yourself. I can't let me get in your way."

"At this point, I don't care." He said. "I want you to live more than I've ever wanted someone to, because I don't want to be without you. Is that horrible?"

"Timothy, Mr. Logical, you do know you will hate yourself in the morning for saying all this, right?" I tried to peer into him the same way he did to me.

Timothy put his hand in my hair. Love and want crept across his lined face. He pulled my head toward his. Our lips met and he kissed me deeply. I kissed him back. I was in trouble, at that moment, I knew there was no doubt that I loved him.

Max murmured something in his sleep. It intruded upon our moment. We both glanced over at the couple next to us. Max didn't move but I saw that his fingers clung to Cara for dear life.

I directed Timothy back to me. "Give it a chance, for them." I shrugged. "They have found a little hope in each other. It's not so bad to see your sister happy, is it?"

"No." He answered. "I want to protect her. She's been through a lot. She still hurts from not having a normal life; one that isn't clouded by other people's agendas."

"Has she ever been in love?" I treaded carefully on the subject.

"Not that I know of." He speculated.

"Max seems like a good first love for her. He seems innocent enough and I don't think he will hurt her on purpose." I said.

"Are you a good first love?" His eyes twinkled in the dim light.

"I'm your first love?" I gasped.

He bit his bottom lip. He was slightly embarrassed by his confession.

"Probably not in this world." I frowned. "I'm clumsy, jaded from loss, and the camp drained years from me. I had way too much time to think."

He grinned. "I'm a great catch myself. No family or friends. All I have is a tiny shack on the seashore. My job is dangerous and I'm a wanted man by a conquering nation of genocidal earth dwellers."

I giggled and leaned forward to kiss him lightly.

"Do you think they are gone for the night?" I changed the subject.

"Not sure, they may come back to do a final sweep before heading back." He grimaced. "I'll stay awake to keep an eye out."

"I'll keep you company." I offered.

I knew it was a lie as soon as I said it. I dozed off in seconds.

A new dream came to haunt me. Timothy ran into Max's house after we heard the gunshots. I heard another shot and pushed the front door open.

Max's dad shoved me down and fled upstairs. There were more gunshots above. I recovered and ran into the living room.

Timothy stood over the bodies, his back to me. I put my hand on his back and whispered his name.

He didn't respond. I rounded him, to find him wide eyed with his hand over his heart. He lifted his hand and blood sprayed all over me.

"Alex." He croaked.

He fell and I went down with him. I tried to cover the gaping hole in his chest but blood poured out.

The blood began to burn my skin. It was like acid on my flesh. I screamed and scratched at my arms to get it off. It blistered my arms. I felt it seep through my face and neck.

"Run!" Timothy gurgled.

My eyes shot open. I grabbed for Timothy. I moaned with fear. He was there, instantly. He scooped me into his lap and rocked. I abruptly realized that I was crying. Strands of my hair stuck to my face in sweat and tears.

My fit woke Cara and Max. They rose and wiped their eyes from sleep.

Cara crawled over to me. The sun was still beneath the horizon. Her white eyes searched mine.

"How does it feel today?" She asked about my cut.

"It feels much better." I breathed.

Max scooted over to have a look, as well. Cara lifted my stained shirt. The stitches were prominent against the white of my skin. A small amount of dried blood caked the area. She plucked the blood away to inspect the wound thoroughly. The dried blood flaked away. It revealed a clean stitch job. The cut itself was purple, because it healed greatly overnight.

Max leaned over Cara's shoulder. "That is truly amazing. I've never seen anything heal like that."

“Don’t let her fool you,” I bragged. “Cara is a remarkable healer. If it weren’t for her, I’d be dead a few times by now.”

“She also did a heck of a job fitting the aluminum to my soles.” He boasted and lifted a foot for me to see.

Cara blushed fiercely. “Well, someone had to do it, since Timothy gushed over you the whole time.”

It was Timothy’s turn to redden. “Come on, Alex was hurt pretty bad. I was worried.”

“Alright, alright.” I intervened. “Thank you, both, for taking care of Max and me.”

I pinched the bridge of my nose and shot Timothy a glance. I hoped he would read my face. The others needed to know about the soldiers during the night.

He slightly nodded at me in understanding. “We had company last night. A few soldiers came through while Alex and I were up. They passed back through about two hours ago. I suspect they were heading home.”

“They came through here and you didn’t wake us up?” Cara asked. She was angry.

“You guys were sleeping soundly. I figured if I woke you, you might make noise.” Timothy explained.

"Cara, when I saw them, they were armed. We couldn't have fought them. It was better to lay low." I defended him.

"Soldiers, you mean from your kind?" Max said harsher than was meant.

"Yes." We said in unison.

"Um, sorry honey, but we forgot to mention that we killed a few people before we met you. They don't like us much right now, with the deserting, saving humans, and killing them and all," she said sarcastically.

"Whoa." Max raised his hands in surrender.

"Take it easy, Cara." Timothy demanded.

"Okay, I'm alright with doing away with a few human killers, so relax." Max said darkly.

I shuddered because I knew Cara better by now; that was the wrong thing for Max to say. She was the kind of girl that talked tough but would prefer to not hurt anyone.

Cara huffed and moved away from him. She started to gather things around the platform. She even cursed a few times to herself.

Max appeared at a loss for words. He could tell that Cara was upset, but had no idea why.

Timothy gave me a meaningful glare.

I mouthed. "It will work out."

Cara ignored Max and watched Timothy.

"What do we do now?"

"We get to the boat and ride it up river to the next settlement. I have a few things left to trade so I'll get us some weapons. A crossbow would've come in handy last night."

"Does the boat have an engine or are we rowing?" I needed to prepare myself if it was the latter.

"It has a small engine that won't attract too much attention, but will add some speed." Timothy said. He dropped the vine from the platform. "Alex is going down with me. Are you guys okay to fend for yourselves?"

It came off as a challenge to them. Could they figure it out? Could Max hold his own and maneuver down the vine?

"I'll go after you two and spot Cara." Max proposed.

Cara snickered. "Maybe I should go first to spot you?"

I shook my head. "Max, you have a lot to learn about Cara."

"It seems so." He sized her up.

Timothy positioned me on his back. My side still ached, but it was tolerable. He inched his way down the vine and set me down on landing. We both turned our faces toward the platform.

Cara and Max grabbed the vine. Cara stared him down.

“Come on, let me be the gentleman. Let me worry about you some.”

Cara paused and released the vine. She sighed. “You know all I’ve ever wanted was someone to do that for me. Here I am fighting with you over the opportunity.”

Max grinned from ear-to-ear. “Thank you for letting me.”

He grasped the vine and wrapped his legs around it. Cara held the vine steady. He lowered himself to the ground.

Timothy placed his hands on my waist. He rested his head on my shoulder as we watched them.

Cara winked at Max. “Just don’t expect me to be your damsel in distress.”

She tucked her hands in her sleeves and slid down at a rate that made me gasp. Max caught her at the bottom.

“Good lord, you’re a feisty one.” He grinned and pecked her on the lips.

Timothy and I marched ahead.

“You were right.” Timothy said.

"One way or the other, they will figure it out." I confided. "Just like us."

He cocked his head at me. I stuck my tongue out at him. I had thought about how things would be if it didn't work out between us. I hoped to never find out. However, the logical side of me reasoned that if we fell apart, we'd figure it out.

Each of us took the stone field to the water our own way. Timothy stepped confidently and pulled me along. Max bounded over them like an animal. Cara looked a lot like a tightrope walker. She kept balance with her arms out at her sides.

Our group made it through the rock obstacle unscathed. I think we all breathed a sigh of relief. No casualties, yet, today.

Timothy promised that the boat wasn't too far down river. I walked on the pebbles and mud with his hand in mine. He kissed the top of my hand and an electric sensation ran through my body. I wouldn't want to be on this journey with anyone else.

Chapter Twenty-Five

At a point where the river bed expanded, Timothy let go of my hand and walked to the trees. I followed him to a place that the ground was sunken, covered in leaves.

"If anyone happened upon this, they would think this was a trap and avoid it." Timothy kicked back the leaves to reveal a flat board. "Help me lift it." He told Max.

They peeled back the board to reveal a boat hidden beneath. They propped the board against a nearby tree. The boat was humble, large enough to fit our party of four and worn with time. A small outboard motor hung from the back.

"Geez, you guys thought of everything, didn't you?" Max wondered.

"We've been going after people for years now. So, you learn how to make things as comfortable as you can." Timothy responded. "It's going to take all of us to lift it, minus

Alex. It's not a good idea for you to lift the weight with your sutures. I could do it myself, but it's an awkward shape."

"Really?" I shoved my hands in my pockets. "I can't help?"

"No." Cara cautioned, "Timothy is right. If you tear the wound back open, I'll only be forced to use more of our meds. Plus, it'll hurt really bad and all."

"Fine." I sighed.

I stepped back and watched the trio strain to lift the boat onto the ground. They placed it upside down before they rolled it right side up. Cara dropped down into the hole and tossed up two oars. I plucked them from the edge and dragged them along to the shore where the boat was being pushed to the water.

Max panted with exertion. The rest of us took notice. "You guys have got to remember I've been held up in that house for a long time."

Cara motioned for him to come near. She looked concerned. "It's probably nothing, but I need to take a listen."

She placed her ear on his chest. "Your chest sounds clear of fluid, which is good." She stepped back and looked in his eyes. "Have you ever been diagnosed with asthma?"

Max smoothed his shirt over his stomach.

"When I was a kid, but I haven't had a problem with it since." He shrugged.

"Ok, well, you are having a problem now. Sit down and try to relax." She directed.

He followed orders. Cara sat with him and talked him through breathing. She slowly massaged his shoulders and upper back.

Timothy and I exchanged glances. At least it wasn't what his sister had. Timothy shoved the boat the rest of the way on his own.

Eventually, Max's breathing got under control. Cara wrapped an arm around his waist. She guided him to the boat. It swayed as she climbed aboard and she directed Max to sit in the bottom near her. I balanced myself and sat on the other side to give them space.

Timothy shoved the vessel, splashed through the shallows, and hopped in. He settled next me.

"I'm going to use the oars for a while. The boat makes traveling faster but it also leaves us out in the open. We don't need to attract attention." Timothy explained. He notched the oars and began to push us through the current.

"Let me know when you get tired and I'll take a turn." Cara offered.

"Me too." Max piped up.

"The heck you will," Cara responded.

"Come on, Care. I need to build my strength back up."

"Maybe for a little at a time." Timothy approved.

Cara nodded at me. "You should be healed up by nightfall. I'll take out the thread then and you can take a turn."

I was relieved. "Good, because I hate feeling useless."

Timothy turned the oars over and over. The rhythm made me sleepy. Cara and Max snuggled. The pet name Max had called Cara made me smile. I dozed in the sun and allowed my eyes to close.

I was nudged awake. My eyes were blurry from sweaty sleep. The sun felt warm for once. I forced my eyes to focus.

Timothy pointed ahead. Above the river bank was clear of trees. A large wagon sat on the precipice. The wooden wagon was haltered upon two horses. Slats raised around it, like a paddy wagon. A shadow moved inside. A pair of hands shot out between the slats. They waved frantically.

"Help, help me!" A woman's voice cried.

I turned to Timothy. "What is going on?"

Max and Cara were asleep in the bottom of the boat.

He pulled me near. "It's a trap."

"What? Why?" My heart lodged in my throat. The woman's screams continued.

"She's bait." Timothy said in a solemn voice. "Either she's with the trappers or she is their prisoner and they put her there to attract people."

"That is sick." I stated. "There is nothing we can do, is there?"

He shook his head. "Anything we try will end with one of us in that cage."

As we neared, she became more frantic. The woman beat on the inside of the enclosure and yelled with all her might.

Cara rose and took in the scene. She shook her head. "Poor thing, if she is a prisoner. I hate when they do that."

"Obviously, you have seen this before?" I asked.

"Yeah, she is there to lure people to her and there is an ambush set up." Cara warned. "When we were new to rescuing, we found that out the hard way. We were lucky to escape alive."

"What do the trappers do with their prisoners?" I was afraid to ask but curiosity got the best of me.

"Everything you can imagine. Women are used and then sold as slaves or taken to our people for a reward. It depends on whether the trappers have a relationship with our people. Men are used as slaves or turned in also." Timothy said scornfully.

As we gained distance, the woman's voice ceased. I looked over my shoulder to see that two men had appeared at the river's edge. They watched as our boat moved away.

"Luckily, they don't have guns or we'd be in trouble." Timothy explained.

Max stirred and moaned. His forehead was beaded with sweat. Cara felt his head. She nodded at us to explain that it was just the heat. She woke him and made him shed his jacket. The rest of us followed suit. Out in the open, the sun warmed us quickly.

Cara passed out the last of our meager rations. I fed Timothy his food so that he wouldn't have to stop rowing. The current was very slow.

The day slipped from us. The sun hid behind the trees. The river expanded to almost fifty yards across. It was peaceful and didn't seem to be as rocky.

Cara leaned over the side of the boat. She was looking for decent size fish. She asked for the grocery bag I found last night. I handed it to her. She poked several small holes in the bottom. Then she tied the handles to her knife and trailed it in the water.

Soon, she had a brim snared and plopped it onto the floor of the boat. She neatly held the bag and sliced the head from it. She tossed the head back into the water. She was a genius as far I was concerned.

Max looked on and took note of her technique. I could appreciate his willingness to learn. After she caught a second fish, he offered to try. He was jumpier than she was. He hauled up a twig or big leaf a couple of times. When he finally got the hang of it, he produced a fish in the bag. Max copied Cara's slaughter of the fish. He beamed with pride.

In the late afternoon, Timothy rowed us to the shore. "I need to be very careful about where the boat is stored."

"What are you thinking?" Max questioned.

"How about I take the oars for a while? Cara said I should be ok by now." I intervened.

Cara disagreed. "Let's stop here for a bit and cook up these fish before they go bad. Then, I vote for Alex's plan. I'll take over after she gets tired. I don't think it's a good idea to cook and eat where we are going to sleep. The fire and smells might attract company."

The boys agreed and we made land. Timothy jumped out and ran the boat onto shore near a fallen log so it wouldn't drift away. It was nice to stand and stretch. Each of us rubbed out our stiff muscles.

The boys built a fire. Cara cleaned the fish, she taught me as she worked. In no time, they had a spark fostered. They cradled it in kindling and blew softly on it to persuade the fire to grow.

Cara spiked the fish through several times to ensure that it wouldn't fall from a stick. She roasted it on the open fire the boys had made.

Each of us received our piece, in turn. We sucked the meat from the bones noisily, tossing the remains into the woods. I licked my fingers to retrieve the last morsels of nutrients left behind.

It was a fine meal, but nowhere near enough to fill my belly. I realized then that my stomach ached from hunger. There had been so much going on that I had not listened to it.

The rations at camp were meager, but there was usually some kind of grain included. The biscuits or flat bread stuck to your ribs longer than meat alone. I couldn't believe my mouth watered at the thought of camp food.

Cara interrupted my thoughts; she insisted on the removal of my stitches. That was one way to forget about hunger quickly.

Cara worked on my side. She used the light of the fire to cut one of the knots at the end of my wound. My fingers dug into the dirt with every pull of the thread through my skin. It hurt so badly because the skin had completely healed around the stitches. The tiny bit of salve worked too well.

She apologized over and over for the pain I experienced. I grit my teeth until I was sure I would break them. I was careful not to make any noise, even though I vibrated during the procedure.

Chapter Twenty-Six

At the end of our stay, Max kicked dirt over the fire. Our group loaded back into the boat. Timothy slid the boat away from the shore.

I blinked and two men ran out of the trees. “Stop right there!” One of the men bellowed.

With a jolt, Timothy shoved us away from him with all his might. The boat skidded to the middle of the river.

I gripped the edge of the boat. “No!” I yelled at both Timothy and the men.

Cara leapt for the motor and pulled on the string to start it. Timothy raised his hands. The men walked to him. The motor sputtered. Max grabbed the gun and cocked it low as to not give it away. The motor whirled again and sprang to life. Cara turned us back toward Timothy.

The men held knives; no guns were visible. I whispered that to Max. The motor was so loud the men couldn't hear me. Unfortunately, I couldn't hear what they were saying either.

Timothy was turned toward them, hands still raised. The men yelled at us over the noise of the engine to shut it off. Cara did as they asked, but took the oars to keep us aligned with them. We were far enough from the riverbank to keep us safe.

"Pull the boat in, honey!" One of them commanded.

Cara turned the boat and slowly oared us toward shore.

One of them jerked Timothy's arm down behind his back. Timothy quickly turned on the man. He swept the man's feet out from under him. He pounced on the other man and punched him square in the jaw. The man fell to the ground. The first man started to recover, but Timothy struck an elbow on the back of his head. He crumpled to the ground.

Cara returned us to shore. Max sprang from the boat and joined Timothy.

"Those were the guys from earlier. They must've followed us." Timothy announced.

"That means the wagon and the girl are nearby." I concluded.

Timothy nodded. As soon as I could jump to dry land, I did. Cara stayed on the boat.

"Should we look for her?" I proposed.

"What do you think?" He directed at Cara.

"Go, but make it quick. Max and I will watch these guys."

Timothy grabbed my hand and we ran up along the embankment. The wagon was there just as predicted.

The woman reached out to us. "Thank God. Did you kill them?" She asked. She ran to the back of the cage.

"No, so you better tell me now, are you with them?" Timothy shot back.

The woman wailed. "You have no idea what they have done to me. Please, please let me out. I just want to get back to my family!"

Timothy climbed up the wooden cage and released a bolt holding the back door locked. It fell open. I held out a hand to the woman and she collapsed onto me. We landed in a heap.

Timothy pried her from me. Her stench consisted of bodily fluids and grime mixed together.

"Thank you, Jesus, thank you." She stumbled away from us. She picked up speed with each step. Then she disappeared among the trees.

A gunshot fired, another followed. The blasts echoed from the river. I froze. Timothy reached for my hand and pulled me into a sprint. Down the bank and below we ran.

Max laid face down; the gun lay beside him. The two men were on the ground in odd angles, blood pooled around the one nearest to Max.

I searched for Cara. She was crouched in the boat, her eyes wide. Timothy rolled Max onto his side.

"I didn't have another option." Max cried.

"It's okay, you did what you had to do." Timothy reassured him.

Max curled into a fetal position. Timothy cradled him in his arms. Timothy whispered to Max and tried to soothe him. Max's muscles were rigid as though his whole body had cramped.

I trudged into the water and entered the boat. Cara's eyes didn't leave Max. I wrapped my arms around her.

"What happened? You don't get like this." I spoke in a soft voice.

"He didn't have to." Her voice cracked.

"What do you mean?" I asked.

"He didn't have to kill them." She blinked. "The one guy surrendered when he came to. He shot him anyway. Then, he shot the other. He was still unconscious. He didn't have to."

The thought sank in. Max had killed them without warrant. I knew she made a connection between his actions and those of his father's.

I reasoned the situation in my mind. Max had to be scared. He might have reacted irrationally. Had they deserved to die? I saw what they did to that woman. If they had lived, they would've done it again. They would've lured people into their trap for their own gain. The world might be a better place without them.

"Cara, if you had been with us-." I changed my angle midsentence. "What these guys were doing was sick. The wagon was up there. The woman had been taken. I can't even imagine what they put her through."

"It's not that he shot them, Alex." She trembled. "It's that he changed. He went blank. I called to him. He didn't look at me or say anything. He was like a machine. It scared me. After what his father-." She stopped.

"Cara, we need to hear Max's side of the story. I'm sure he was terrified." I said convincingly.

"Alex!" Timothy called out. "Get the oars notched. The sound of those shots traveled."

I did as I was told. “Let Max explain when he is better.”

Timothy hoisted Max over his shoulder. Max was still crippled by what he had done.

Timothy laid him in the bottom of the boat. He hugged his knees to his chest.

Timothy sat down and took the oars from me.

“I’ll row first; I can do it faster.” He advised.

He plunged the oars into the water and we sprang forward. He moved us with the speed of his full strength. The tiny motor had nothing on him. The breeze lapped at my face.

Cara stared at Max as though he was a vile disease that had crept on to the boat. She didn’t seem to know what to do. It’s hard to avoid someone in such a small space.

“Did he say anything?” I tilted my head to Max.

“He said he snapped. He wasn’t going to let them hurt Cara. That was the only thought he had.” Timothy barely moved his lips as he spoke.

“He will need to tell her that.” I decided.

“I have a feeling that he hasn’t killed anyone before.” Timothy speculated. “His dad may have taken care of the dirty work till now.”

That was a reasonable assumption. A father would try to shield his child from that weight.

The memory of my own dad tugged at my heart again. He would expect me to take care of myself; but if he was there, he would've taken matters into his own hands.

I leaned onto Timothy's back and held him around the waist. I rocked with his movement. My father would be happy that I had someone to help me, to keep me safe. My eyes clouded with tears. There was so little time to heal out here; there was always another situation to deal with.

I had all the time in the world to think at the camp, but I had always pushed emotions down. I feared weakness there.

I peeked around Timothy. Cara had rested her head in her lap. Max was still motionless on the floor.

Not so long ago, I had taken my first life. I had done it to protect Cara and Timothy. It still hurt; I sympathized with him.

When he finally began to relax, I crawled over to him. I held his hand. He peered sideways at me.

"It's ok, Max." I whispered. "We've all had to go through this. Whether you had to or not, you did it because you didn't want them to hurt anyone else."

He squeezed my hand. “Then why do I feel like a monster? Why does Cara look at me like that?” He stammered.

“You have to tell her why. Right now, she doesn’t understand.” I explained.

Timothy started to breathe heavily from exertion. “Alex, I am about ready to hand it over to you.” He puffed.

I took my spot between the oars. “I say we take turns through the night.” I rationalized. “There is no sense in stopping to run into another issue. I think we should skip stopping at the next settlement. Do we have enough supplies to make it?”

Timothy pulled the knapsack open and rummaged through it. Finally, he nodded in agreement.

Chapter Twenty-Seven

Timothy moved over to Cara. He hugged her and allowed her to rest her head in his lap. They were beautiful creatures. I wished cameras still existed, so that I could capture their sibling moment of tenderness.

Timothy spoke to her in a hushed voice. He told her about the woman we found.

Cara's demeanor relaxed with his words. He knew his sister best out of all of us. I knew he could calm her.

Darkness enveloped us and a fog covered the water. I was thankful for it because it would help shroud us from anyone on the banks. It was difficult to see too far ahead of us. I took this as a lucky sign.

As time passed, Max sat up. He turned to Cara. She also roused from Timothy's lap. Timothy took this as a sign to give them some space. He made his way back to me.

"Are you holding up alright?" He asked.

"Honestly, I'm getting sore." I confessed.

He took the oars from me. He jumped right back into the pace I had set.

"Will she be okay with it?" I questioned.

"Yeah, once he gets around to explaining it himself." Timothy reckoned.

Max asked Cara if he could sit by her. She scooted over to put some space between them. She looked exhausted from the day.

She listened as he spoke. He reached for her hand and she allowed him to take it. Cara melted into him. I believe the thought of him going blind to right and wrong for her was ultimately attractive to her. Her brother had been the only one to love her. Now she had to adjust to letting Max love her, even though he might not always show it the right way.

"Alex." Timothy muttered. "We are going to be nearing another compound soon. One like you came from."

My breath caught in my throat. "What? Why didn't you tell me?"

"I didn't know how you would react. I decided I couldn't keep it from you any longer." He sighed.

"Tell me about this place. Are we going to be in danger?" I panicked.

"We will be passing by in about an hour. Hopefully, this fog will stay and help keep us hidden."

"What do they do there? You said each compound has a different function," I recalled.

"This one is a farm. They grow plants and livestock to feed the other camps." Timothy said.

"Is it run like mine?" I felt sour that he kept this from me. My stomach clenched from nerves.

"It is similar in the way they use humans as slave labor. The biggest difference is its size. It is huge. As you can imagine, it takes a lot of food to keep things running. They even provide some of the food for the underground communities." He glanced at me.

"How many people do you suppose are there?" I grew angrier.

"I'd say upwards of a thousand."

I huffed at his response. I tried to imagine the scale of the camp. It was unfathomable.

"I will have to tell Max soon, too." Timothy relented. "I hope he can handle it since he has had such a rough day."

"He doesn't have much of a choice, does he?" I said sharply.

"Please don't be angry with me. I wanted you to not worry about this on top of everything else," he confided.

I sat in silence. I wanted to be mad, but how could I? In his own way, he tried to protect me in a way I didn't think was right, which is exactly what I had hoped Cara would see with Max.

"Be real with me, what are we up against here?" I realized I sounded like Cara.

"Depending on their alert status, we range from not a concern to we need to be ready to fight." He closed his eyes. I took it that Timothy feared the worst.

"You are killing me." I shook my head at him. "We have one gun, an incredibly loud outboard motor, and are about to pass a high security compound. Tell me if I'm wrong but that seems like our odds are ridiculous."

"Like I said, if this fog stays thick, we should be okay." He grew impatient with me. "If you have any ideas, please, share them."

I crossed my arms. "You better break it to Max, soon. How's that for an idea?" I snorted.

I scooted away from him and sat on the floor to sulk.

"Max, if you can't tell, I have some bad news to break to you." He gestured to me. He went on and repeated the situation to Max.

As Timothy talked, I realized that I trembled. I was scared. I had every right to be. We ventured into enemy territory. I tried to talk myself through the anxiety that swelled.

It was foggy; that was in our favor. On the water, they could not track us on the type of radar the moles used. There was the gun, it offered little protection if we were bombarded, but at least, it was something. Lastly, I was with Timothy and I knew he would have my back.

At the end of Timothy's debriefing, I saw Max's eyes focus on the gun in the bottom of the boat.

"Let me take over rowing for a while. You need to be ready to get us past there, fast. I don't think I'll be able to take the gun, not this soon. Please, can someone else do that?" He requested.

"I'll do it." Cara volunteered.

"Okay, so we have a plan?" Timothy replied.

Everyone looked at me. "I guess we do." I shrugged.

Max made his way to the oars. Timothy stretched his arms and moaned in release.

"How long will it take you to get us past the compound?" I asked Timothy.

"Maybe fifteen minutes or so," he said delicately.

I groaned. Fifteen minutes was going to feel like a lifetime.

"On a good note, they haven't built a bridge over the river, yet," Cara added.

"Gee, great." I rolled my eyes.

Cara lifted the gun and inspected it. She checked the magazine and loaded it with the remnants of ammunition Max had brought with him. She appeared to have enough to load once more, if needed. That was the end of it.

Timothy shuffled over between Cara and me. "Only shoot if it is necessary. If they can't see exactly where we are, firing will give it away."

She nodded in response.

"There is no other way around?" I questioned.

"Timothy is right, unfortunately, the compound stretches the river. Either way around would be even more dangerous. We are safest in the water; our kind rarely know how to swim. We only learned because of necessity in this business." Cara smirked in defiance.

One more thing to add to our list of advantages, I noted.

"To go around by land at a far enough distance, might add several more days." Timothy revealed.

"Okay." I succumbed to our route.

"When we get close, you and Max will stay low. Let us handle everything. Stay quiet, no matter what." Timothy commanded.

He grabbed my hand and drew me near. His hands gripped the back of my neck; he kissed me hard. This time was different than before, it was hurried, even a little desperate. He wanted to remind me of how he felt.

He turned his head into my shoulder. "I love you. I am sorry we have to do this."

I kissed his cheek. "I know." I paused. "I love you too. You better not get yourself killed, because I'm really starting to get attached to you."

Timothy lifted his face to meet mine. "Say it again." He begged.

"What the part about not getting killed?" I giggled.

He kissed me and spoke between my lips, "The other part."

"Oh, you mean the, I love you part?" I moved my lips against his. He pressed his lips into mine again. The kiss went on for a few seconds and I broke away first. I could feel Cara and Max watching us.

"Dear lord, you two!" Cara teased.

"Get over it." Timothy spat back.

Max laughed and I blushed while I still held on to Timothy. He was my anchor in our journey. At least, Cara and Max had each other.

Chapter Twenty-Eight

We sat in silence and waited for the inevitable to come. Cara leaned over the side of the boat and watched her fingers trail in the water. Ripples formed beside us in the black water.

Timothy held on to me, tightly. He caressed the tops of my hands with his thumbs. Every so often, he paused to kiss them.

Max rowed steadily ahead toward the place that might very well determine our fate. The air became heavy. We traveled this way for a while.

"We better get ready." Timothy announced.

He plucked his contacts from his eyes and stored them in their case. Cara followed suit and removed her tinted contacts once again.

Each of us carried out the beginning of our plan. Timothy climbed back to rowing position. Max relinquished duty. Max moved to the middle of the boat and stopped to quickly give Cara a peck on the lips and a hug. I sank down below the sides of the boat. Cara curled herself around the rifle. She barely peeked over the edge to stay as hidden as much as possible.

"If you need me to take over, I can do it." Max said to Cara in support.

"If I need you, you'll know it." Cara replied.

My heart beat in my ears. Adrenaline filled my body with nowhere to go.

I turned on my side so I had both Timothy and Cara in my sights. That way, I could spring into action if either needed me. Both siblings had their brows creased in concentration.

My ears tuned into any sound that caught my attention. I waited.

It would be after work hours at the farm, so most would be back to their shelters by now. I forgot to ask if the guards were human or of their kind? It would make the difference between being spotted in the dark or not. I silently cursed myself. I should've asked.

Timothy rowed quietly, but with long strides. He winked at me and gave me a smile. I closed my eyes and took a deep breath. I just wanted this to be done.

Cara swiveled her head from side to side. She watched both sides of the river. It was difficult in the fog to make out the shoreline or the trees beyond. I hoped the same would be for anyone that kept watch.

Muffled noises greeted us. Light peeked through the fog and darkness. The light of fire flickered and flashed along the tree line.

Timothy stiffened at the sight. His reaction made me shudder.

Voices carried from the shores. I couldn't make them out, but several men spoke and the sound struck me rigid.

Cara was on high alert. She turned from side to side and kept an ear out for any sign that we had been seen.

I saw sweat drip from Timothy's jaw. He had such a strong jawline. I traced it with my eyes. If we made it through this, I promised myself to make sure I kissed it. His arms flexed, then released. Every moment was savored; we were still alive.

The voices continued. The water rumbled beneath us. I looked to Timothy, his eyes pierced mine. Another rumble came. I reached for his ankle.

A Roar followed, it was deafening. I covered my ears, my eyes squeezed shut. It didn't travel through me, but crippled me with its volume.

Once I could bear it, I squinted at Timothy. He seemed immune to the Roar. He rowed faster than he had before. I noticed that he had turned on the engine, to help propel us. Timothy used the Roar as a distraction, in our favor.

He shut off the engine once the noise of the Roar wound down.

I looked back at Cara. She held Max's hand with one hand and the gun with the other. I repositioned myself and pried Max's fingers from hers. I nodded at her to signal that I would handle him.

Max's whole body shook. He was back in a fetal position. I took both his hands and pulled him into me. He was terrified.

"Shh, shh," I whispered. His eyes were wild.

"Keep it together, Max. Look at me."

His eyes focused on mine. "I can't. I can't do this."

"Yes, you can. Focus on me. We will be through this soon. Just hold on a little longer." I coaxed.

"I can't do this, Alex. I'm not meant to be out here. I should've stayed. I should've stayed at the house. Maybe, Cara and I, we could've been something there." Tears streamed down his face.

"Cara." I said sharply. "Give me the gun. You need to talk to Max."

She handed me the gun and slipped into the floorboards. I took her position. I tried to keep my eyes on the shore, but the exchange between Cara and Max grew louder. I put my finger to my lips and motioned at them. It only seemed to spur Max to become louder.

"I can't do this anymore. I can't. I'm sorry." He shuddered.

He tried to wriggle free of Cara's embrace. She clung to him with panic.

The people on the river banks must have roused. Shouts echoed back and forth. I swiveled from side to side. I tried to decipher the movement of the figures. I only saw shadows that ran back and forth in the fog. My finger rested on the trigger.

Max became manic. He told Cara once more, "I'm sorry." He pried himself from her. He looked at each of us and said. "I can't. You are stronger than me."

He jumped from the side of the boat. The splash was loud. More people yelled from land.

The boat plunged to the side. It listed hard. I leaned against it, I saw Timothy do the same.

Cara clamped her hands over her mouth to muffle the scream that came. I kicked Cara hard to knock her down and then spun around, waiting for gunfire to come.

Max swam away from us, back upriver. I assumed, in his madness, he thought he was going back home. Then the gunshots rang, not at us, we still moved downriver, but toward the splashing sound Max made. The bullets sprayed water as they hit the surface.

I turned to Timothy. He shook his head in dismay. There was nothing we could do for him. They didn't shoot at us. They shot at Max and he would be caught or killed.

Cara pulled herself to the side of the boat. She saw the river pummeled by bullets and reached out, and sobbed. I was afraid she would pull herself over to go after him.

I laid the gun down and wrapped my arms around her waist. I pulled her back to the floorboards. She fought me. She kicked and hit me, all the while, logical enough to stay quiet.

Once I had her pinned beneath me, I rose to survey the scene. The bullets still pierced the water but any sign of Max had ceased. A dark red circle stained the surface of the water where I last saw him.

Panicked, I glanced at Timothy, his head was lowered. His eyes concealed; he knew Max was gone.

Cara struggled to the side once more. She kicked my stomach to reach the edge. She saw the crimson water and went slack. I pushed her back down into the boat.

I slumped down into the boat and used my own weight to hold Cara down. I had no more strength to fight her or anyone else for that matter.

I sobbed as I sat on top of her. I straddled her waist, to make sure she didn't try to jump in again. Her body writhed and heaved under me. All I could do was hold on to her and keep her from the same fate.

The chaos on the banks continued. Orders were being given to retrieve the body. A canoe was pushed from the shore.

Selfishly, I hoped they thought he was a lone traveler. That hope was answered with a cease fire. Either, we hadn't been seen, or they were only directed to shoot at movement. Timothy rowed in near silence.

Timothy kept his pace; his head hung between his arms as they pumped. His strength came from somewhere within.

That was when it dawned on me why I loved him. He had an innate will to go on, despite any situation. He would always push forward.

His will to survive inspired me; it made my will stronger. I would make it. I had to, to prove the odds wrong.

Maybe the thing in my leg would set us all free. I rubbed at my shin with the thought. I was thankful the object had been tolerable.

In spite, I wept for Max. Cara was heartbroken, unable to acknowledge me. I laid my head on her shoulder and held her under me. Her pain reverberated through me.

Hours passed with us this way. Timothy finally wore out and directed us to shore. The darkness of the night was thick, but we were beyond the danger of the compound.

He stepped out of the boat and pulled the boat onto the rocks so that we wouldn't drift away. Timothy came into the boat and positioned himself so that he could wrap himself around both of us. An arm was placed around Cara and I was against his side. He gently kissed his sister on the head and held her hand, as she continued to cry for her lost almost-love.

I pushed myself as close as I could into his side.

I laid an arm over him to comb my fingers through Cara's hair. She didn't seem annoyed so I took that as a sign that it soothed her. I knew pain; I knew what it was like to lose. Empathy poured through my strokes. Sadness enveloped all of us and squeezed our hearts.

How do you make this better? Cara had seen hope with Max; hope is a dangerous thing in the new world. I feared it would callus her further.

She had opened a door to her heart only to have it brutally slammed.

We all knew Max was weak from isolation, but to do this, to give up on her was the gravest form of betrayal. Her mind worked through these thoughts, also.

We lay in the boat and drifted off at times due to the exhaustion of mourning. The sun rays reached over the horizon to cast long shadows in the forest behind us. Timothy squeezed my hand and pulled me to Cara to take over.

He met my eyes and nodded to tell me to not let go of her. He left the boat and went ashore. His footsteps echoed lightly as the leaves and dirt crunched.

Cara still sucked in hiccups, but she appeared to be asleep. I nestled into her warmth. I hoped I provided her some. She flinched every so often in her dreams. I feared what they might be. I had seen the red water, where the bullets had hit Max and I knew she did too. I tried to push the memory from my mind.

Timothy rocked the boat when he stepped back inside. Cara sat upright and looked around. She grabbed at me. Her eyes were wild with fear. I grasped her shoulders until her eyes focused on mine. She searched my eyes for answers. When she saw, I had none she broke down.

"How could he do that?" She cried upon my shoulder.

I hugged her tight. Timothy sat on the other side of her; we encased her body.

"Cara, Max had been through a lot. He just couldn't live with it." Timothy said.

"I could've been enough, if he had given me the chance." She moaned.

"You could've been but he didn't hold on long enough." Timothy answered.

I held on for the anger I knew was coming. Cara was strong. She would mourn for Max, but eventually she would become angry. Max hadn't been strong and that would make her angry when she came to terms with her sadness.

"You guys don't have to hover over me. I'm not going to do something stupid." She sniffled.

"Ok, but we aren't going to leave you completely alone." I said.

Timothy and I released her. Cara fell onto her back and stared at the sky above. We left the boat for land. My feet sunk into the muddy water. "What in the world happened?" Timothy asked.

"He just lost it. He kept saying I can't do this over and over. Then he said if we had stayed at the house, he might have had a chance."

Timothy held me close while he kept an eye on his sister. He kissed me on top of the head. The smell of him made me relax. I needed that.

"You know Cara best, is she going to be alright?" I spoke into his chest.

"I think so, she is strong." He sighed.

I sat on a fallen log. "He wasn't." I closed my eyes.

Timothy sat next to me and his dark hair fell over his eyes. "No, he wasn't. I hate that he couldn't be for my sister."

"Have you lost people before?" I pried gently.

Timothy folded his hands in his lap. They were bloody. I pulled them so I could have a better look, but he recoiled and shook his head.

"Yes, they were never people we had become close to. There were people we tried to save, but they couldn't be saved. People like Max, too conditioned to live only in their previous environment."

"I don't know how you've done this for so long." I wondered and I tried to imagine.

"Today, I'm wondering the same thing." Timothy remarked.

I kept a close eye on Cara. She positioned herself to watch the water. Her stillness contrasted the rest of the world that went about its business. Birds flit from branch to branch, the clouds over head steadily passed, and the breeze dropped leaves to twist in the air.

“Timothy, let me look at your hands.” I demanded.

He gave into my stern voice and held them out for me. They were raw and blistered from the wooden oars.

“I didn’t know I was gripping them so tight.” He mumbled.

“I’ll wrap them. Maybe Cara has some cream we can spare.” I hoped.

I turned his hands over and kissed them.

“Please don’t make a big deal about it to Cara. She has enough to worry about.” Timothy urged.

I dug around in her bag for the vial and something to wrap his hands. I nodded in agreement.

Chapter Twenty-Nine

I didn't want to disturb Cara. She seemed so peaceful by herself in the boat.

The boat bounced upon our entrance. I shuffled through the pack and looked for anything I could use to wrap Timothy's hands and some medicine.

Cara didn't acknowledge me. Her face was blank except for the tears that stained her cheeks. I found what I wanted and stepped around her to return to Timothy.

He held his hands out for me to apply a small amount of the medicine that was left. I was careful not to use it all. His wounds weren't deep but I wanted to ward off infection. I tore a shirt into strands and tied them around his palms. His fingers weren't in bad shape so I left them free for him to use.

Timothy decided that he would keep watch with the gun. My station was at the oars until I tired. I resolved to push myself beyond my normal threshold for Timothy's sake. At this point, we needed to count on ourselves so Cara had as much time as she needed.

My leg stung. It reminded me that it was still a problem. I had ignored the irritation and apparently, it felt neglected. I massaged it quickly and then rowed.

It was a gorgeous day just to spite us. In every book or movie, I could recall, it was always a gloomy day when someone important died. The sunshine and birds sung to mock our mood. The river was less rocky which allowed the water to sweep past, calmly.

"I should've known better." Cara broke her silence.

Her profile was visible since she was turned sideways in the bottom. She blinked slowly.

"I should've known better." She repeated.

"Cara, you took a chance on someone. That isn't a bad thing." Timothy said soothingly.

"It sure feels like it was." She crossed her arms on top of her knees and rested her head upon them.

"Don't shut down like that." Timothy pressed his lips into a thin line. "Did you care about him?"

“What kind of question is that? Of course, I did.” Cara growled.

“Then remember what you both gained from it.” He advised. “What’s done is done, but you cared about someone for a little while. How did that feel?”

Cara scrunched up her face. I braced myself for her to lash out. Instead, she surprised me and a smile played at the corner of her lips.

I eyed Timothy and silently cautioned him not to push it further. He grinned at me, proud that he had been able to lift Cara’s spirits.

I feared the anger. I knew it would come from her. It was only natural to go through it after a loss.

I remembered my own anger at the Roars and the moles when they took my family. There was anger that swelled inside of me when they took our things.

In the beginning, the Roars made me want to rage, because it took our freedom of choice. It was all a part of the process, to weed out those that could become numb and those that couldn’t. I wondered if that made me weak or strong?

Timothy waved at me to snap me out of my own thoughts. He pointed at Cara. She had drifted off to sleep.

He took the pack and retrieved the grocery bag Cara had used to fish. He peeked over the edge and dragged it in the water. Several times, he jumped before the fish was deep enough in the bag. I giggled softly. He grimaced and stuck out his tongue at me.

Luckily, he got the hang of it and scored a decent dinner for us. Five small fish laid beheaded on the bow of the boat. He gutted them and threw the innards back in the water.

Cara stirred and stretched from her nap. She looked around to get her bearings. Her eyes rested on me. She probably hoped it had all been a nightmare.

Reality hit and her face sank.

"Timothy caught us dinner, Sleeping Beauty." I offered.

"What is that?" She asked.

"Well, there's fish and more fish. Take your pick." I joked.

"No, I meant Sleeping Beauty. What is that from?" She continued.

"Oh, it's a story. It's about a princess that is cursed by a wicked witch that makes everyone go to sleep for a long time. Then a pr.-" I trailed off.

I stopped myself. What an idiot, with the whole prince kissing and saving part. I cursed myself silently and blushed.

"Go on, I want to hear it. Even if my prince was a weakling and dove to his death, doesn't mean all stories have to end like that." Her voice was sour.

I looked to Timothy and he shrugged.

"A prince came along and kissed her. The whole kingdom awoke from the curse. The witch came back to defeat them all, as a dragon. The prince slayed her and they all lived happily ever after."

"They all lived happily ever after?" Cara whispered. "What kind of crap is that?" She raged.

"It's a dumb story." I agreed.

Cara huffed. "What a complete load, right? There is no happily ever after. There should be death at the end of every ever after. That is everyone's outcome, right?"

"Cara, I'm sorry. It was a stupid reference. All the silly fairy tales people came up with end like that. I didn't mean to-."

"Hold on." She interrupted and held up a hand. "All of your stories end that way?"

"Well, they aren't my stories," I exasperated. I dug my own hole.

"No wonder your people are so weak. You people tell stories that end that way. You do some stuff, meet a prince, and live happily ever after." Cara cried.

Timothy interjected. "Cara, calm down."

"Wait. I'm not done." Cara grit her teeth. "I'm out here saving the princess. Where's my place in the story? Is there ever a prince's tag along sister? I bet not, because she's at home waiting on her own prince to show up and do his duty. Then if they get lucky, they get old and nasty together. Probably end up hating the sight of each other and die. How's that for an ending?" She glared at me.

"Cara." I started.

"Save it." She grumbled, "I'm so glad you found your prince. Just don't count on the happily ever after junk."

"That's enough." Timothy jerked her arm.

"How dare you." She punched at him.

He restrained her.

"That's enough," he growled.

"Really? You are going to do this? You are an idiot, too." She strained against him.

I dropped the oars in case he needed my assistance. Cara struggled against him. Timothy's hand wraps came loose. His hands smeared blood on her arms while he held her tight. She looked down and saw the bloody handprints on her. She slumped in his grasp and sobbed uncontrollably.

He laid her down. "Are you done?" He asked.

She nodded through her cries.

"No more fairy tales." Timothy said scornfully.

"I'm sorry." I apologized.

Timothy's face softened.

I picked up the oars and continued to cry quietly. I am an idiot, I thought to myself. Maybe there was some truth in Cara's rant. We were pumped with those cheesy stories and reality could never live up to them.

Chapter Thirty

After the fall-out, Timothy announced that we had one more day left in our journey. I should have been happy, but the unknown scared me.

He told me that we would stop for the night, soon. We would have a place to stay. He was still short with me, but I relaxed since I knew the end of rowing was near.

I had pushed myself much further than I imagined possible. My arms burned, but they turned in a robotic motion that only my mind controlled. I didn't dare ask for reprieve since Cara's meltdown.

She stayed curled up among the floorboards the rest of the day. She barely moved. She only flinched in her sleep.

Timothy scouted the trees and the banks along the river. He listened intensely to the noises around us. He made himself look very busy.

My leg screamed so I stretched it the best I could while I rowed. It didn't go unnoticed that he didn't offer help, either. My shin throbbed and more than once, I felt a trickle of warm blood run down into my boot. I didn't have the gumption to say anything to the others.

Finally, Timothy pointed to the shore. I rowed to the spot he directed. He pulled us aground. I stood, each vertebra popped, and every joint crackled. I limped from the boat. Timothy scooped up Cara in his arms.

"I'm going to take her down first. We have to pull in the boat."

I followed him away from the river. In the side of a slope, Timothy kicked dirt from the side. There was an indention that looked like a handle. He nodded at me to pull it. I yanked and a small wooden door cracked open. I used my hands dug it free.

It looked like an old bomb shelter. The inside was cemented and round like a silo that had been put into the side of a hill. He crouched to walk in and I did the same. A few feet inside, the ceiling opened and we could fully stand. Timothy placed Cara on a cot and waved me back to the entrance.

"We need to stow the boat over there." He pointed to thick brush encased by a circle of trees.

We dragged the boat up as far as possible. I remembered this was a job for three people so the two of us needed to compensate. We hoisted the boat over our heads and waddled under the weight. I asked several times for a break.

Timothy grew irritated with me. I didn't like his new attitude toward me. My normal reaction would be to give it right back, but I knew that wasn't going to get me anywhere.

The boat was lowered into the bushes. Timothy placed branches to envelope it. I stepped back to fully appreciate the camouflage. No one would ever see it, unless someone stumbled directly upon it.

"I'm going down to sweep away the drag marks." He abruptly turned away from me.

I caught his shoulder as he passed. "Come on, you know I didn't do that on purpose."

He pinched the bridge of his nose. "I know." He took a deep breath. "What you said hurt her. And what she said back had some truth to it."

"Yes, it did. We are weak, overall. That is why your people have conquered us. I get that. Our arrogance and unfounded belief that we ruled this Earth got us here.

However, that isn't you and I, we are here and living. I would like to spend any time I have left facing this God forsaken place with you." I shrugged. "The only humans I've run into out here are animals."

Timothy looked me square in the eye. "No fairy tale needed?"

"Are you kidding me?" I stomped. "Look around us, I want to survive. I want you and Cara to survive." I cautiously reached for him.

He fell into me and wrapped his arms around me.

"Surviving is good." He spoke into my neck.

"It's definitely better than the alternative. I never hoped for princes or magical sunsets to ride off into and I never will. For one, I'm not an idiot." I savored his body close to me.

"I didn't think you were. It's just that I can't live up to anything remotely like that. Trust me, I'm not a prince." His lips caressed my neck.

I chuckled. "I only want us to live. Everything else is a bonus." I squeezed him.

The pain in my leg stabbed sharply and I folded. Timothy held me upright. He took a step back and looked down at my leg, it was bloody. He immediately picked me up and carried me to the underground shelter.

Cara was still curled in a ball on a cot. Timothy nudged it as he past. "Cara, get up. Alex's leg is bleeding."

Timothy laid me on another cot. Cara sat up and blinked herself back to reality.

"I need to stop the bleeding." He said to her.

She glanced at me and begrudgingly pried herself from her resting place. "Listen, I know you've been through a lot. Alex and I both understand. However, she needs you. Please." Timothy begged.

She shuffled over to me. I rolled up my pant leg. It exposed the old, dirty dressing she put on a few days ago, soaked with blood.

She gasped. "Alex, I am so sorry. I didn't realize it'd been so long since I checked it."

She scampered around the small room to find the bag.

"Timothy, I'm going to need a fire and boiled water." She instructed.

Timothy put his hand on her back. "Thank you, I'll get it going. I need to brush down our tracks too." He turned and exited the shelter.

Cara carefully sat beside my legs. She peeled back the cloth over my shin. I winced as it pulled dried blood away from the wound.

"Why didn't you say anything about your leg?" She asked wide-eyed.

"You've been a little busy." I shrugged and laid back.

"This is no joke. You could have an infection setting in." She scolded.

She felt my forehead for fever. Her facial reaction revealed that it wasn't good.

"It didn't hurt that bad." I lied.

"I'm sorry, for what I said in the boat. I lashed out at you because you were an easy target. It wasn't fair of me to say those things."

"I expected you to get angry at some point." I admitted. "I guess I didn't think it was going to be directed at me, but I expected it." I grinned, despite the pain.

"One day, I will ask you about the fairy tales again." She smiled at me.

I shook my head. "You'll have to take that up with Timothy. I promised no more fairy tales."

She grunted. "I need to make peace with him, too." She sighed. "I'll go, get things ready. I can't do anything without the water anyway." I covered my face and nodded.

When I peeked between my fingers, she was gone. I lifted myself to get a good look at my leg. The light was dim and it made it difficult to see. I could tell that the blood on the bandage was caked with crusty blood and dirt. My leg seemed to be in the same condition as the bandage. I hovered my hand over the wound; heat radiated from it. I knew that was a bad sign.

I wiggled my toes and a shock ran through me. I gripped the sides of the cot. A strange movement under the skin occurred.

When I dared to try it again, I forced my eyes to stay open to watch. Immediately after my toes stopped, the same shock spread through my body. This time, I saw a long cylindrical shape protrude under the skin and then it slowly receded.

"Cara!" I called.

Both Timothy and Cara ducked inside. "Are you ok?" Cara rushed to me.

"I think so, but this is new." I nodded to my leg and held on to the cot. I moved my toes and the same thing happened again.

Their eyes widened. "It looks like it is trying to work its way out!" Cara exclaimed. "We have to get her leg stable, now."

Timothy ran from the shelter and returned with hot water. Cara cleaned the bloodied area. She scraped away the dry crust and more blood seeped out from the top and bottom of the cylindrical shape.

"Timothy, I need you to get me things to make a splint. She's can't move her leg below the knee anymore." Cara instructed.

"Got it." He squeezed my hand and left.

Cara continued to clean my leg. Her brow furrowed with focus. I placed my hand on her arm and she tried to smile at me. She was worried.

"Timothy told you we only have one more day, right?" She said.

"Yeah, I'm glad." I responded and sank back down on the cot.

"Me too, you better hold on till then. This guy we are meeting seems to know what he is doing. He will patch this thing up."

"How do you know?" I asked.

"When he first came in to our village, he asked around looking for us. He knew what we do. I met with him. He explained that there was girl that was going to be carrying information that might end all of this. This man claimed to be on the team of doctors that put this in you." She paused.

"He did, but how?" I probed. "I don't even remember them doing it."

"It's the Roar. They can erase things with it, that's how they were going to move you. You would never even remember it. They chose a human to transport it because there have been some issues with rebels below.

Some of the people down there don't think that what is happening is right. If one of the rebels were to find the capsule underground, they would have control or they could sell it to the highest bidder. Whatever is in your leg is very important."

"I can't even wrap my brain around this. So basically, I was going to be used as a transport?" I choked on the words.

Cara nodded. "The doctor said that he had been recruited as a surgeon. He spent the past several years gaining the trust of my people. He knew that it would allow him certain privileges, such as information.

Once they implanted the device inside of you, he escaped. He made his way to us so that we could find you."

Timothy entered with several smooth pieces of wood. He laid them next to Cara.

"Will these do?" He asked, hopeful.

Cara turned each piece over. She nodded. "I have one more request. I need you to pull apart the other cot."

Timothy eyed her. "What for?" He asked.

"Outside," she said as she dragged him out.

I could hear muffled voices as they argued, beyond my sight. When they returned, Timothy glanced at me sympathetically and he dismantled the cot.

Cara walked over to me and took my hand. She opened her mouth to speak.

I interrupted her. "I know what you have to do. Just do it."

Cara bent and kissed me on the cheek. "It's your turn to yell at me." She smirked.

I frowned. "I'll try my best to refrain."

Timothy handed Cara a leg he had recovered from the old cot. He took my hand from her.

"I'm sorry, Alex." She apologized in a whisper.

"Are you sure we have to?" Timothy grumbled.

Cara nodded and went outside. Timothy handed me his jacket. I twisted it and put it in my mouth. I didn't want to break my teeth.

She returned with a red-hot iron. Timothy laid his body across my chest. Cara put her weight on my legs.

Then the burn came. It seared through my body. I screamed into the jacket in my mouth. Then the pain subsided for a moment and returned at the other end of the capsule.

I smelled my flesh as it burned. The pain was inconceivable; blackness circled my view. It overwhelmed me and I passed out.

Many hours later, I awoke. Timothy was next to me in the cot. His arm cradled my head; his fingers entwined in mine. His eyes popped open. He stared into my face. I grimaced at the pain I still felt. It wasn't like before when Cara's medicine took the pain away.

"Cara used the last of her concoctions. It didn't take the pain away?" He whispered.

I shook my head. I bit my lip and held back a scream from the pain.

"We were afraid of that." He breathed deeply.

I tried to bury the pain. I closed my eyes.

Cara's story about the man that paid for me, echoed in my mind. I wondered how much of it Timothy knew.

"Talk to me?" I pled. "Tell me about the man that paid for me."

Timothy took another deep breath. "I never met him. We always think it's better for one of us to remain anonymous. Cara told me about him; he was a surgeon and that you were to be relocated with the device intact. The device holds information that can be used to make things better for your people."

"Do you know why they chose me? Out of all the people at the compound? I remained quiet. I did what I was asked, and that ended with me to be used as a transport?" I said softly.

"They probably chose you because of those reasons. Alex, I'm not going to let them do anything that will take your life. I promise you that. I've already decided part of the deal will be that I am there when he takes it out," he promised.

"Why can't Cara do it? Couldn't she sneak into the village, get the supplies she needs, and do it?" I proposed.

"I asked her the same thing. She is afraid that the capsule might be too close to major blood vessels or nerves for her to do it. She doesn't want you to bleed out or have permanent nerve damage." He kissed my shoulder.

"How does it look now?" I asked.

"There is going to be scarring. The man will deal with that to get to the capsule. If he put it in, he should be able to pull it out."

My body felt like it was on fire. I writhed from it. Timothy gasped and pulled me close to him. His chest pressed against mine. I panted as the pain subsided some.

"Timothy, this is getting too much for me. I don't know if I can take it." I wept. I seized with another surge of pain.

Timothy climbed over me. He woke Cara.

"We have to go. She is hurting too much." Timothy spoke harshly.

Cara sprang from the bed and felt my head.

"She's burning up." She announced.

"Let's get the boat and go." Timothy said.

They went outside. Their voices were muffled but the concern resonated. Cara came back in and grabbed her pack. Timothy lifted me into his arms. He kissed my lips gently and we were off.

I was laid in the boat. I felt it rock when we took to the river. The sky above was dark, only a sliver of the moon was visible. The motor started up and Timothy took the oars.

I blinked and shivered. It was the first time I had been cold in days.

Timothy said something to me. I couldn't hear him over the motor, so I just nodded. I hoped that was the right response. Darkness closed in and my eyes became heavy. I allowed them to sink shut.

Cara woke me, later and made me drink. I was drenched in my own sweat. I needed to stay hydrated. At least the sweat meant I broke a fever.

Cara took the oars and Timothy came to me. He placed my head in his lap and gently caressed my face.

"Stay with me, ok?" He whispered as my eyes shut. I forced them open. "Please stay awake a little while."

"Then you've got to stop touching me like that." I coughed.

"I keep daydreaming or in this case wake-dreaming about when we get home. You are going to love it. I can't wait for you to feel the sand and the ocean against your skin." He said wistfully.

"Will you go swimming with me?" I asked.

"Of course, I will." A tear streamed down his cheek.

Panic struck me. He cried because he didn't know if we would get the chance. I realized how bad it must be. I gripped his pant leg, if I held onto him I would stay alive.

"Don't let me go, Timothy." I begged. Tears blurred my vision. "There's too much to do."

Flashes of what could be haunted my thoughts. "I won't give you up easily, I swear," Timothy choked. He held my hand to his lips and gently kissed it. "You are right, there is too much to do. I have too many things left to share with you."

"I love you." I mumbled sleepily.

"I love you, too." He shuddered.

He bent forward and enveloped my face with his hands. He kissed me deeply. Timothy smiled down at me, his dark eyes oceans of want and hope. "Too much of that left too."

I nodded and bit my lip. He traced the features of my face again. My leg tugged at me and I winced. He kissed my forehead and soothed me with his touch. I drifted off in another wave of fever.

Chapter Thirty-One

I peacefully dreamt of the ocean. Timothy and Cara splashed among the waves as they giggled, and dove beneath the waves. I lounged on the sand and enjoyed the sunshine on my skin. My fingers wriggled into the cool sand. As I closed my eyes, I licked my salty lips.

In the sand, my fingers bumped into something hard. I turned over to face the ground and brushed away the sand to uncover the object. A finger was uncovered. I gasped with fear, but tried to pry it free. It twitched and a whole hand grasped my arm. I screamed loudly.

Hands jutted from the sand around me, they clawed, and scratched at my skin. I turned to see Timothy and Cara as they ran toward where I was pinned. I struggled among the hands.

They pulled me down into the sand. My skin tore from a hundred fingernails. I sunk down till my knees and arms were beneath the surface.

When Timothy reached me, he kicked at the hands. A few of them let go. He yanked at my shoulders and screamed. Cara pulled at my waist. It was no use, they had a hold of me beyond what could be seen.

The skin tore, especially on my leg. The hands wasted no time and pulled the capsule from me. The rest of my body was disposable.

I shot upright. I heaved from my dream. The pain in my leg didn't subside. It felt like the capsule wanted to force its way out.

I screamed. "Help me!"

Timothy held my leg and pushed back the pants.

"Cara!" He cried. His face was panic stricken.

She climbed over me. I felt pressure; it made me scream louder.

"What?" I writhed. "Tell me!"

"It partially made its way out," Cara cried.

"Get it out!" I yelled. Sweat from fever and pain stung my eyes.

"I can't Alex, it's like I feared. It's embedded in the muscle. If I start pulling it out here, it can permanently screw you up, big time." She stammered.

I felt pressure again near the exposed capsule. The pain entered my brain and made the outline of my vision black. I screamed until I was hoarse.

I heard Timothy yell at Cara. His voice was muffled in my head. Another poke to my leg followed. My face contorted. I felt like my whole body was ripped open. Then I blacked out.

Chapter Thirty-Two

"It's Timothy and Cara!" Timothy bellowed.

My eyes half opened. My vision was tunneled. I tried to make out the shoreline.

Timothy waved his red jacket over his head. The sputter of the engine pounded in my skull. Yells echoed from the shore.

"Tell the doctor to get ready now!" Cara screamed.

I blinked.

My body lifted from the boat. I felt Timothy's arms around me. My head bounced from the jolts as he ran. Beads of sweat dripped from my brow.

I caught glimpses of people in my peripheral vision; hands covered mouths or gaped at us. Timothy shoved past people in the street. Roofs passed and the smell of smoke tickled my nose.

I turned my head and vomited.

Timothy didn't pause. I could feel his heart pound in his chest. My eyes rolled into the back of my head.

"Stay with me." Timothy panted.

There was a surge forward when he kicked open a door. He stumbled into a makeshift hospital room. Timothy swept his arm over a table which cleared it and laid me down.

"Doc!" Timothy yelled.

A short, pudgy, middle-aged man materialized from behind a curtain at the end of the room. The man adjusted his glasses and clasped his hands together. He looked down upon me.

"And here she is." He was clearly astonished at the sight of me. "Thank you, you may go, young man."

Timothy shook his head. "I'm not leaving her. You are going to get that thing out of her and save her." Timothy protested.

"Now, that wasn't part of the deal." He grabbed a pair of scissors and cut my pant leg away.

"It is part of the deal now. If you don't, I swear, I will break your neck with my own hands." Timothy clenched his fists.

"I thought you were more professional than that. "He scratched at his ragged beard and narrowed his eyes.

Timothy left my side and rounded the table. "Don't you dare chastise me for not being professional, you moron. I will make sure that when I break your neck it looks quite professional." Timothy raged. He pushed over a table with utensils on it.

I gathered my strength and raised my head. They stopped and stared at me. The doctor looked at me over the top of his glasses.

"Please." I gurgled.

The doctor held my stare for a moment. He huffed and threw his hands in the air. I dropped back onto the table.

"Give me a minute. I'll need a few more things."

Timothy returned to my side and put his hand on my forehead. He traced the lines of my face with his fingers.

"It'll be okay, I swear it." He promised again.

The doctor returned with a needle and a cart of supplies in tow. He pushed some liquid from the syringe. Then he plunged it into my arm, roughly.

Their voices became murmured. There was a blur of movement. Timothy and the doctor melted into dark shadows. The pain dulled into an ember. The light of the room dimmed from the anesthetic.

Chapter Thirty-Three

I smelled him before my eyes opened. Timothy's hand held mine. My fingers twitched between his.

"Get the doctor, now!" Timothy yelled.

Footsteps shuffled in response.

Timothy held my hand to his mouth. My eyes focused on his face, which scrunched, and he sobbed. He kissed my face over and over. His tears wet my cheeks.

"I made it." I whispered.

Timothy paused and lifted the upper half of my body into an embrace.

"You did. Thank you, you did." He cried.

I noticed my surroundings were not the same as the room the surgery was conducted. I lay on a soft bed with sheets. They felt like heaven.

The room was bright despite the wooden walls. A few dried herbs hung from the ceiling near the door. Vases held bright wildflowers, scattered around the room.

Timothy blushed. "I couldn't go far so I made myself busy."

"How long has it been?" I licked my lips.

Timothy held a small cup to my lips and poured water into my mouth. It ran along my dry tongue. I forced myself to swallow past the knot in my throat.

"About five days." He replied.

"Mmm." I moaned.

My head sank back against the pillow. That seemed like a long time to be sedated.

"It was complicated, the removal. Then the doctor had an extensive infection to bring you back from." Timothy nuzzled into my neck. "How does your leg feel?"

I shrugged. I slowly bent my knee to test it.

"It is sore but nothing compared to before." I said.

The doctor rushed into the room. He didn't even knock. Timothy regarded him with a nod and stood back to give him room.

The doctor pulled a stethoscope from his pocket. "Hello, my dear. Let's have a look at you."

My face reddened and I cursed. "I haven't forgotten that my living was of no matter to you."

He eyed me and said, "You weren't in good condition when we first met. I apologize for my demeanor. I've never been known for my bedside manner."

"No kidding." I spat.

Timothy interrupted. "Alex, try to remember that you are here because of Doctor Jameson. He worked hard to save you."

I chuckled. "I'll try to keep that in mind."

Doctor Jameson listened to my heart and made his way around my body. He poked and prodded at me.

"Well, I'm glad to say that Timothy will not be breaking my neck anytime soon." He tucked the stethoscope back into his pocket. "I suggest that she stay in bed for at least another day. Then, she should be able to move around more easily. Did you make the crutches?"

"Yes." Timothy smiled and retrieved them proudly for us to see. They were hand carved, quite beautifully, in fact. The wood was polished and smooth.

"Good job young man. I am going to head back to my lab. I am still trying to figure out how to run electricity to the device in this God forsaken place."

"I will be able to help with that as soon as I get her on her feet." Timothy remarked.

The doctor nodded in appreciation. "That would be welcomed. Your sister has been trying to secure a generator for me but she is turning up empty handed.

It is of upmost importance that I get the plans from the device soon. I fear that your kind will try to replicate it, quickly, especially if they gave up on finding her." He motioned to me.

He told us to come find him if any difficulty arose and left.

Timothy crawled into the bed and held me tight. He kissed my forehead. "You have changed everything."

Epilogue

Timothy walked beside me as I hobbled. It was hard to use the crutches in the sand. As good of a job as Timothy did, I hated them. I had used them for a couple of days now.

Cara procured more of her healing cream upon our arrival at the camp. She gave me a vial and told me to apply it to the incision once a day.

I secretly limped around without the crutches when no one was looking. Cara's healing concoction worked wonders. Still, Timothy insisted that I use them.

Cara ran ahead, over the small dune. She beckoned us to move faster, but gave up on my slow struggle to the beach.

I would be scarred for life from the burn and the surgery. I was happy with the battle scars. They reminded me of how far I had come from the camp where I had been a slave.

At the summit of the dune, we paused. My eyes widened at the beauty of the ocean. My hopes paled in comparison to the expanse before me. The blue of the water was majestic. The sand stretched for miles in either direction. The salty air blew my hair away from my face.

Timothy rounded me and wrapped his arms under my shoulders.

"This is gorgeous, but there is nothing like the look on your face at this moment. I will remember it forever." He said dreamily.

He kissed me and lifted me into his arms. He carried me closer to the shoreline.

My senses were alive in this place. The sounds, the smells, and the waves calmed every fear I had. I felt the release I had waited for.

Cara ran down to the water. She stripped her clothes and splashed in the shallows. I giggled at the coarse girl I knew. She behaved like a child.

Timothy placed me on a sheet that Cara had spread on the sand. He sat next to me and took it all in. Timothy waited to come to the beach until I could join. He wanted to experience it with me this time. We both sat in silence and savored our riches.

After a while, Timothy rolled on to his side to face me. "Since I got the generator from the next settlement, Doc says he will have the encryption figured out in the next couple of days." He sighed. "I've been talking with him about what to do with the information inside of the capsule."

I bowed my head. "Something tells me that involves you in some way." I peered at him between strands of my hair.

He nodded and reached for my hand. "It does, but I've been rallying a few guys to join me. They are going to start training with me tomorrow."

"That doesn't leave me much time to get rid of these things." I pointed at the crutches.

He shook his head. "Whatever we decide, I can't take you."

"I'm not asking you. I won't let you go without me." I said sternly.

He looked in my eyes and opened his mouth to protest. I raised my eyebrows at him. He closed his mouth. We locked stares in a silent stand-off.

"I can do it. In a couple days, I'll make sure I can. If I can't walk without the crutches, you win." I bargained.

Timothy gave in to me. He knew this was a war he wouldn't win. Secretly, I hoped he didn't want to leave me either.

"Timothy! Timothy!" A small boy charged at us from the dune. "Doctor said come, quick! He was able to break the code!"

We looked at each other in shock.

"Come on!" The boy darted away.

The Roar Trilogy

The Roar

Book One

Into the Roar

Book Two

Above the Roar

Book Three

About the Author

A.M. White lives in Wesley Chapel, Florida with her family. A.M. White was inspired to write, The Roar series after she moved to Wesley Chapel, because she experienced a phenomenon often reported in the community. Residents post on social media about a “boom” that shakes buildings and the ground. So far, there has been no confirmed explanation for the events.